MW00444885

Advance Praise for

BAD MOTHERS, BAD DAUGHTERS

"I loved the stories in *Bad Mothers, Bad Daughters* with my whole heart, thrilled by their intuitive leaps of imaginative logic, their celebrations of wonder and surprise, and their centering of the unbridled wildness of the mind. Maya Sonenberg has given me exactly the kind of gift I want from a collection of stories: precisely made, gorgeously rendered worlds, each so inventive that it suggests there's always even more magic waiting beyond its margins. I know I will visit these stories again, and that next time they will transport me even further into wonder."

—Matt Bell, author of *Appleseed*

"Maya Sonenberg's contemporary tales are alive with the pulse of the mythic, and her fairy stories brim with all the light and longing of the everyday. These visions of mothers and daughters—broken, breaking, seeking, striving—stick in the mind even as they open the heart. What a powerful, gorgeous collection."

—Jedediah Berry, author of *The Manual of Detection*

"Maya Sonenberg's *Bad Mothers, Bad Daughters* is a revelation of fairy tale and form. In gorgeous, clear prose, evoking a playful range of settings—seascape to castle to hospital room to Seattle landmark— Sonenberg irreverently questions the loaded roles of child and parent, of princess and witch, of caretaker and abandoner, all the while piercing the wonders of both our natural world and our labyrinthe hearts."

—Sharma Shields, author of *The Cassandra*
and The Sasquatch Hunter's Almanac

"The luminous sentences that comprise Maya Sonenberg's *Bad Mothers, Bad Daughters* house one surprise after another, never landing where the reader expects linguistically, narratologically, or existentially. They delineate quietly broken lives and unhurried regret in fictions that exist within beautiful clouds of ontological static."

—Lance Olsen, author of *Skin Elegies*

"Maya Sonenberg's witchy and yet touchingly vulnerable characters bring to mind the 'bad' mothers and daughters of Lispector, tinted with shades of the Brothers Grimm."

—Barbara Browning, author of *The Gift*

"Written with humor and spirit, this lively assembly of protean fictions takes us from castle to carwash via an anxious activist, a frazzled painter, a pickle maker, an exemplary whale, and the always illuminating chimpanzee."

—Rikki Ducornet, author of *Trafik*

Bad Mothers, Bad Daughters

THE RICHARD SULLIVAN PRIZE IN SHORT FICTION

Editors
William O'Rourke and Valerie Sayers

MOTHERS

DAUGHTERS

Bad

Bad

MAYA SONENBERG

University of Notre Dame Press

Notre Dame, Indiana

University of Notre Dame Press
Notre Dame, Indiana 46556
undpress.nd.edu

Copyright © 2022 by Maya Sonenberg

All Rights Reserved

Published in the United States of America

Library of Congress Control Number: 2022935740

ISBN: 978-0-268-20301-6 (Hardback)
ISBN: 978-0-268-20302-3 (Paperback)
ISBN: 978-0-268-20303-0 (WebPDF)
ISBN: 978-0-268-20300-9 (Epub)

for

Ezra and Phoebe

Alef and Tav, Sun and Moon, Noon and Midnight

CONTENTS

ACKNOWLEDGMENTS

Many thanks to the journals in which many of these stories first appeared, some in different form: *Conjunctions, Dark Matter: A Journal of Speculative Writing, DIAGRAM, Fairy Tale Review, Lady Churchill's Rosebud Wristlet, The Literarian, New Ohio Review, Pacifica Review, Pear Noir!, Requited Journal, Seattle Review, Signs of Life, So to Speak, Upstreet, Western Humanities Review,* and *White Whale Review.*

"Moon Child" was written in response to artwork by Yevgeniya Beras and Teresa Baker shown at the Alice Gallery, Seattle, WA, in October 2015. Thanks to Julie Alexander for commissioning the story.

The title of "Inebriate of Air" comes from Emily Dickinson's poem 207, "I taste a liquor never brewed," which inspired the story.

Unending gratitude goes to the University of Washington's Helen Riaboff Whiteley Center where many of these stories were written and to John for keeping the home fires burning.

Bad Mothers, Bad Daughters

Childhood

"When did the dark come in?" she wonders, looking at the photograph. Self-possessed, she spun on a beach in Oregon. She wore a tie-dyed dress and flung her arms wide, sleeves and skirt belling, vibrating yellows, blues, greens, pinks. She was ten years old, alone on the sand. Deliciously, she was smiling. Now she feels she has broken through all the childproof gates, avoided child labor, survived childbed fever, and grown up, only to face, astonished, in this one telescopic moment, herself as a child, but it's not the same child she remembers.

Her own children ate jelly beans. The boy savored the spicy ones: red-hot cinnamon and grayish-purple clove, the color she imagines photons to be. The girl hoarded hers, pink ones, white ones even if they tasted of coconut, counted them and counted them again, smiling. After giving some to her mother, she saved the rest for herself. Then she changed her mind, gave some to her brother, and they made a home for the candy in an old bucket they painted blue. On summer afternoons, the children sat under a tree by the street and sold their wares, all the candy they had saved together all year.

Of her childhood, she remembers: dark winter afternoons in her friend Silly-Milly's bedroom, darkening Barbie dolls with Magic Markers until they wore a variety of black and purple bruises. Then, she just thought it was a weird form of decoration, but now, a mother, she thinks of them as bruises and is aware, too, that if she weren't a mother, she might just think of them as tattoos. Her friend's home was strange—that was the prevailing sensation. At dinner, she was served half an avocado with vinaigrette pooled in the center, its texture unbearable, something dense

3

like liver, something smooth and slick like the glossy surface of a photograph. Now she loves avocado, slices it onto whatever whenever, but for years it didn't seem like something she, herself, would ever like. She remembers the next time she ate it, snuck inside a turkey sandwich when she visited California, and how she smiled, surprised at its *goodness*.

One morning her son dressed in costume jewelry, put on glittery blue wings over his baseball pajamas, a golden crown, plastic rings with smiley faces on every finger, layers and layers of beads. He knelt for the camera in this pool of finery, unaware that it might be the last time he dressed in jewels. Even though he was not yet conscious of self in relation to the world, this moment held future moments and their opposites. As a child, she dressed in Mother's stilettos, her wedding dress, pillbox hat; she's never worn such things again. She took the photo. In it he's alone.

Of her childhood, she remembers: driving through the desert Southwest, far from home, laid out along the backseat of a station wagon, with her hand down her pants. She didn't have a name for what she did, wasn't even seeking a smile or a sensation but just a way of passing time. Did her parents choose to ignore her or were they too busy enduring their own snapshot melodrama to notice, her mother smoking Parliament after Parliament, her father driving with a bag of ice on his head against the heat? She remembers the red-white-and-blue rocket pop that melted down her arm instead of into her mouth until she wore it like a sleeve. She remembers the red earth and the roar of wind at Monument Valley, how the wind just wouldn't stop being wind until her mother finally agreed to go a motel instead of pitching the tent. In the motel room, her body came back into itself, back into sensations other than wind: the day-old yellow jacket sting on her knee, the tingle of air-conditioning, the reassuring sound of Walter Cronkite's voice on the nightly news, the sweet-bitter taste of St. Joseph's baby aspirin.

Her daughter asked, "How could the first person be born? Wouldn't he have been alone? Who was the first mother in the universe?" Smiling, teasing, she asked, "What's bigger—the earth or the universe?" even though she knew the answer. Then, wearing a serious expression, she asked, "What's outside the universe?" Her brother said, "Nothing is outside the universe, the universe is everything," but she persisted, asked for a picture to prove it.

Here, again, are the gigantic rocks projecting upward out of the blue water into the blue sky, and the beach where, self-possessed or selfless perhaps, she was smiling. Of that trip she remembers: fog and the fact that this was the one place along the coast without fog; the rocks alone like angels; the sky wearing a milkiness, as if fog were a diaphanous dress; and her own bright tie-dyed dress. She hadn't remembered the trip, the dancing, until the photo appeared, sliding out from behind another photo, the one from class picture day the next fall, in which she wore the same dress, ripped at the cuffs and neck by then, the day they all forgot was picture day—her hair, in two messy braids, hadn't been brushed, and her eyes were glazed with sleep and embarrassment, and now when her children ask about her childhood, she shows them both photos, the light and the dark.

Pink Seascape

In the middle of the night, the Princess woke up and contemplated what it would be like to govern. She had spent the previous day in bed with a fever, watching all the Hobbit movies. The last one was called *The Battle of Five Armies*, and although no one really wants a battle (except maybe some of the dwarves), they have a battle anyway. Click click click, all the golden elves in the elf army swivel this way and then that, raising their bows in unison. The elf men, along with the elf women, have long straight hair, often blond, and wear a lot of silver jewelry. The elf king wears a lovely silver crown that looks like branches have permanently entwined themselves around his head. "I want that for every day," the Princess had leaned over and told her mother, the Queen. The Queen had said, "Shhh."

The elf king has hard eyes and one of the elf queens goes crazy when she might be able to take the magic ring of power. She looks like a photo negative and her eyes get even harder than the king's and spew blue fire. The Princess thinks that governing might turn you into a Snow Queen just like that, very hard and cold. You might have to be like that. But what if you only governed women?

Here's what she thinks.

She thinks some things might be different if she could govern only women:

- Fewer swords, more hairpulling. She and her sister used to pull each other's hair. They were dark-haired babies and she's sure her sister pulled her hair when they were in the womb together.
- More kisses, but no tongue. Little kisses.

6

- Pudding.
- Catfights. She doesn't know what they are but she's heard the word, and she's only heard the word in association with the pronoun "she."
- More haircuts, more knots, more bloody cuticles.
- More blood, period.
- More books.

She'd like to think there would be fewer battles but maybe they would just be different battles, or the battles might get interrupted for tea. And then teacups would be thrown.

In the morning, the Princess wakes up and thinks "elf men"? What are men? She has only been allowed to see them from a distance.

The fever has broken, her skin feels cool when she rubs her arm, and today she will go sailing. Alone on the bay in her Sunfish. The pink light scatters differently than the longer blue and green waves at the end of the day.

Dark Season

In the North Sea, an island. A mountain. A lake. In the lake, another island, and on the island, a castle, around which the lake forms a natural moat, deep in summer and slick in winter. Across the sea, toward true north, another island, another mountain, another castle.

Dungeon

Once, a boy lived on the island. In the autumn, on the way to school, he stared out the car window and counted all the birds' nests he could see in the bare trees, balancing in a cacophony of twigs. At recess, he kicked a ball around the school yard with his buddies and when it found the back of the net, he shouted, "GOOOOAAAAAAL," the way he heard the announcers do on the Spanish-language soccer broadcasts he listened to at night. He didn't know where the voices came from, but he imagined places where his friends' breath wouldn't steam from their mouths as they ran up and down the pitch, where, standing between the posts and waiting to dive or punch away the ball, he wouldn't need to slap his hands together to keep them warm. His father, the King, usually taciturn, burdened by ruling, sometimes told him of such places, even claimed to have come from one himself.

On the way home in the afternoon, back over the drawbridge, they passed crows and gulls walking hesitantly across the thin sheet of ice that already coated the lake. Soon frogs would settle in its mud. A heron huddled in a tree. "Shouldn't that thing have flown south by now?" the boy asked his tutor. Ducks had pecked the castle lawn clean. The bunnies had dug their burrows deeper. Up the mountain a bear turned and turned and turned in its cave, readying for sleep. A fire crackled in the hall, and cocoa waited in a chipped mug. It was dark when he woke in the morning, dark when he got back home, but each star, each candle was a jewel, each icicle seemed lit from within and the boy was happy.

On New Year's Eve, when the whole family gathered in the Great Hall, his mother and aunts swarmed around him, sparkly as dragonflies in their holiday gowns, and his uncles in their tuxedos stood in ranks like bowling pins, warming their butts at the fire. The boy imagined curling up into a ball and knocking them down. Every year the King told the story of how he had come to be king, and every year the adults laughed and wept over it, but the boy wasn't sure if the laughing and weeping were separate or went together—were they weeping because they were laughing so hard or were they laughing to cover up how much they were weeping?

The King had followed the princesses down into tunnels that stretched below the moat and opened out into the snow in an alley just off the town square. The boy saw a trap door in the floor of their bedroom, a room even now littered with rocking horses and dollhouses, and the sisters, all twelve of them in nighties color coded to match their New Year's Eve party dresses, threw their arms up over their heads as they jumped down into the tunnels, skirts billowing, shiny and bright as a dozen magic flares.

Some nights they went to the Legion Hall and danced, their slippers tawdry by dawn. Some nights, they smoked and drank, then rolled in the snow on the way back home to remove the smell of cigarettes and booze. Some nights, they went to a gym and wore their shoes thin with rock climbing or kicked them off to play volleyball in the heated sand. They'd hike their long skirts up and tuck them into the waistbands of their matching panties, all twelve of them, the perfect number to field two teams.

Every year the King embellished the story: one year the youngest had nearly caught him when he stepped on the hem of her dress; another year when she smelled his sweat; another when his hand inadvertently brushed against hers. He remembered her skin, hot as a pan that has been left in the oven, and how it sent shivers of desire down his spine. He'd recognized this for what it was, but she, only twelve at the time, thought she felt fear.

Now she said, "Remember, I thought you were a ghost."

But you know this story and how it turned out: The princesses stopped dancing and he married the eldest instead. Family and nation learned to put up with him, and he learned to ride a horse, wield a sword, pass judgment on disputes both great and small, and send his navy out into battle—in short, how to govern their small kingdom.

Years later and the boy has finished growing. Or nearly. Even the town has become stifling. His old school friends look at him strangely now that his picture appears next to his father's on the twenty dollar bills, and they make excuses when he hints that he'd like to toss the Frisbee with them or climb the water tower with a six-pack and a bottle of gin. At home, his eleven childless aunts still ask him to paint their nails and braid their hair, still make sure he wears an extra sweater in winter and sunblock in summer. After dinner, they still regale him with stories of the land down below stairs, not a dungeon but a grotto—or a dungeon that they transformed into a grotto, with golden beaches and palm leaves edged silver by moonlight, the diamond clink of ice in their sweet drinks. They treat me like a baby, he thinks, but sometimes when he's studying his geography, memorizing Spanish verbs, or learning just how to raise a scepter or thrust a lance, his mind wanders to that place and he understands how they must have ached to go there. He'll go down there himself, he thinks, or maybe just escape to a bar in town. But no, everyone would recognize him. This is no fairy tale kingdom where a simple change of clothes can construct a disguise. Maybe he needs a bar on the next island over instead?

A deadly spell of upper management seminars, war games, and constantly whining petitioners has been put on him, but his father's advisors tell him that he's privileged to stand behind the throne, to listen and learn. He sighs; he has no idea how to dissipate the spell. Conquer it. But he knows it exists and he knows he has to end it somehow and he suspects that if the princesses went down, he needs to go up.

For years he saw the other island glimmering across the strait. "Not an island," his tutor warned, "a mirage," and pulled out map after map to show him that it appeared on none of them.

His aunts told him stories about it nevertheless: a sorceress lived there who could turn men into pigs; deep caverns there were stuffed full of treasure, just like his stocking at Christmas; two rocks off the coast were always rumbling toward each other and away again, crushing boats between them. But when they told him these stories, their mouths twitched in a way that meant they were trying not to laugh, or he heard their husbands guffaw from where they sat by the fire, reading *The Sporting News* or *Popular Mechanics* or *Psychology Today*, and he knew not to believe them. His youngest aunt, though, he liked her the best, and so, although her story was not really different from the ones her sisters told, he chose to believe her.

"Once," she said, "there was a glass mountain . . ." But you know this story too.

At night, when he rubbed his feet back and forth against the sheets to warm them, he wondered: What wish could the sorceress grant him? What question could he ask her? What was that spell again? And when he was studying his geography, memorizing Spanish verbs, or learning just how to raise a scepter or thrust a lance, he pondered these things.

Finally he wrestled a kayak into the water, rapping its hard orange shell three times for luck as he'd seen his uncles do before they headed off into a storm. "Spirit of adventure, eh?" they'd always said to him. "Want to come?" but until this day he'd always thought, "No. Adventure's not my thing."

Two days before, though, at that strange graying time that passed as midnight in midsummer, he'd caught his father at this beach, slipping out of his royal robes, naked underneath. "Hey!" he called in surprise from the tree line. "Where are you going?" and his father turned and raised one hand in some sort of signal, and the boy saw the ship out there, battleship gray among the white icebergs.

"There," he said, pointing. "The kingdom is yours now, son."

The boy's mouth filled suddenly with rage. "I don't want the effing kingdom!" All he wanted was to taste the cook's daughter's skin. But the water was already up to his father's thighs, and then his father raised his arms above his head and dove perfectly. The next time the boy saw him, he was standing on the deck of the ship, a red-white-and-blue towel wrapped around his shoulders. He waved and disappeared, and the ship disappeared too. One minute the boy had been walking along, thinking about the cook's daughter and the next minute he was king? That was just crazy! And how had his father called the ship anyway—telegraph? Telepathy?

Now, halfway across the strait, the water was still as it could only be at midsummer, and his paddle dipped quietly in and out again. His shoulders rolled. He looked up. Polaris transcribed an infinitesimal circle in the sky above him. He should have run back to the castle, but he didn't and now it was too late. What could he have said? "Dad swam out to a battleship, and then it disappeared—*poof!* I don't think he's coming back." Now, out on the water, his stifling itchiness was gone, replaced by the feeling he imagined skiers had standing at the top of the run before a race, eyes half-closed, picturing in their minds all the curves and jumps they'd soon conquer.

By the time he reached the other island, it was winter. He beached the kayak, tucked a canteen of water inside his shirt so that it wouldn't freeze, and trudged off between cedars and hemlocks and Douglas fir, a tunnel of striated bark and dark branches. Instead of dusk at midnight, he saw only dawn at midday, and he felt grateful that he'd brought a headlamp and had stolen the goatherd's goatskin jacket and fur-lined boots before he left home. His breath, exhaled into the frigid air, crystallized before it hit the ground, ice tinkling against ice. Maybe he heard a hare thumping its way through the ferns or maybe the chatter of a squirrel, but by the time he reached the base of the mountain he realized that all these noises had only been the crunch of his boots in the snow. And that mountain—it wasn't glass but ice! He ran his mittened hand against the slickness, then looked up from dark to dark and started to climb.

The path was steep, yes, but not so steep that he slid back down, not so steep that, come nightfall, he needed to force his claws into the ice just to stay safe as he slept. Instead, it was just difficult enough to make him thankful when he reached the top, thankful for his health and strength and luck and thankful to the woman there who unlocked an iron trelliswork gate, swung it wide, and ushered him into a snowy courtyard and then into a chamber, sun kissed and flower filled and remarkably warm. "I have summoned you," she said. The woman was of indeterminate age, indeterminate size, indeterminate beauty as all beauty is indeterminate, her hair an indeterminate color that he thought must be blond. She wore a robe of bear fur, which she took off and wrapped around him, and only when her warmth touched him did he realize he had been cold.

Some mornings she rose from bed and stood naked before the window, and even though he now knew her hair was gray instead of blond, he thought how he'd do anything she asked. Other mornings, despite the power workouts, grapefruit and kale diets, and Retin-A prescriptions, she huddled over her morning coffee, wearing faded terry cloth, hiding her soft breasts and the loose skin on her neck. She could read his mind. "Those things disgust me too," she said.

At the end of every day, the boy looked over the icy cliff and saw the frozen bodies of her lovers scattered on the snow below. He knew now that they didn't die trying to reach the mountain's top but jumping from it. When he lifted his gaze, he could see the other island across the sea like a mirage. The gate had been locked since he arrived but if he had crampons, he could climb over the wall and down the ice; if he had wings, he could fly back home. Sometimes he tried to graph his life back there, scratching in the snow with a sharp stick, but he couldn't remember how to slice up the pie chart or what the y-axis should measure. What had been the components of that life? Instead of a line graph, he ended up with a scatter plot in which nothing seemed to affect anything else, and so he remained with the sorceress, so much older than he, so stingy now with her sexual favors, so not kind. This was not what he imagined adulthood to be like, and he missed his many aunts who had cheered at his soccer games and reminded him to do his homework. They'd scratched behind his ears and called him their very own kitty cat, but the sorceress insisted he scratch her back and made him grow his fingernails just for this purpose. Sometimes her skin came away, in shreds and clumps and salty flakes, and he thought he could glimpse some other sort of skin beneath. He wasn't sure if she was writhing in agony or in pleasure.

∾

At night when she closes her eyes, she finds herself in Nordstrom, or maybe Bloomingdale's, looking down a tunnel of light at a hand hovering over a pile of neatly folded cashmere sweaters in cartoon colors: neon green, dayglo pink, acid yellow. "That's my hand," she thinks, recognizing the wrinkles, the brown spots, and the neatly trimmed nails. Last season these same sweaters were all the colors of wine—golden Napa Chardonnay, reddish-purple Burgundy, tawny port, a bloody young Syrah, the deep warm pink of a White Zin. She bought them and wore them to shreds, but now those colors are nowhere to be seen, and she seems to have crossed some divide, which means that she can't possibly wear this year's bright young colors, even if the trim crew neck still suits her. She can't move away from them, though, focused intently on her own hand petting the sweaters. The store's usual soft piano music has gone silent, and the relentless conversations between mothers and daughters that usually echo from the dressing rooms are gone too. The first time she met her young lover (the first time they flirted, the first time she touched his arm, the sounds of the winter castle faded to nothing, and the servants dissipated as if made from smoke), she felt this way, as if the world was pulling away from her like taffy. And then a saleswoman startles her: "Can I help you?" She closes her eyes and tears pool behind the lids—lakes filling and filling. When she opens them, she sees the sky, an even spread of clouds clamped down over her like the lid of a pot. Tomorrow, she will let him go.

Four Phoebes

Now listen. Do you see those birds, four of them, perched on the wire? Do you see how they dip toward each other and away again, constantly wagging their tails? Do you see them take off, then spread their wings as they catch their midday meal—the wasp, the bee, the grasshopper, the fly? Do you hear the insistent first note of their call, the soft stutter of the second, their emphatic *fee-bee?*

Any ornithologist will tell you that the phoebe is a solitary bird, more likely to join a winter flock of Eastern bluebirds or pine warblers than to seek its own kind, but these four sit together, fly together—oldest to youngest, largest to smallest, shrinking manifesto of themselves, each with a smaller white patch on its breast sparkling against its dun back and wing feathers. They used to be human, you know, human sisters, but they've been on that wire for six years, six years as birds.

I am going to tell you the story of their kindnesses to each other, how when the third Phoebe was kidnapped by a giant when walking in the forest, the first Phoebe came after him with a wooden spoon, the second wove a net to catch him, and the littlest, the fourth, dressed up as a white cat and followed him home. On the way, she found Number Three's feet, which the giant had chopped off to prevent her from running away. The cat placed these into a velvet sack and took a detour to find the right herbs for a salve. When she found her sister and opened the sack, the feet had turned into birds, white with rings around their necks like the remains of a red necklace, but with a kiss, she was able to turn them back into feet, attach them again to the poor torn ankles, and heal her sister's wounds. How the two eldest saved the youngest from the giant is another story, one about wits and bravery, and perhaps they will tell you that one themselves if you are very quiet and listen very carefully.

The sisters lived in a city perched at the top of a great waterfall.

Yes, cliffs and a cataract, billowing mist, pontoons, bridges, pilings, guy wires and suspension cables, piers, docks, wharfs, and jetties. Above, the sky, and below, the raging waters. In summer, tightrope walkers seemed to float in midair under their red and white spotted umbrellas. Far below, tourist boats defied the rapids, drenching their riders with spray. In winter, amusements sprang up on the banks above the falls— skating parties, bonfires, and sing-alongs—and mountain climbers tried their skills against the rugged, cascading ice.

The girls' father controlled the falls with a golden dial, and they all lived in a castle at the very center of the city, surrounded by mazelike rose gardens, wax museums, and curiosity shops. The castle's portico is crusted with gold and its front door is guarded by a purple demon.

When the girls were still tiny, their mother died and their father re-married. You might think that the constant roar of water would have forced them all to speak louder, but in fact it made them quieter, and they grew up whispering into each other's ears until it drove their father crazy, wanting to hear what they were saying about him, but since they would never tell—there was never anything *to* tell—he turned them out. The castle's turrets grew haunted, and the girls, all but the youngest all grown up by then, moved to an old farmhouse at the edge of town, one with a sagging porch and scabrous clapboards, a tilting chimney, and a weedy overgrown lawn.

The girls had only each other since their mother's death. Father had left her for a blond enchantress. Or did he enchant her? Or was it his gold? Or his crown? Never mind—what's important is this: Mother withered—green leaf, berry, stem—until only the skeleton of the leaf remained and her goodbyes to her daughters were slight as the wind and their father remarried. They carted her cold body home wrapped in white linen and buried her under an apple tree.

The eldest Phoebe was a chef. At home she heated cans of soup and opened bags of packaged salad, wishing she had the time to make her sisters hearty meals of plump meat-filled dumplings floating in rich chicken soup, crisp potato pancakes shining with oil and dressed with sour cream, carrots braised with honey, chopped liver mixed with chicken fat. She hated to see them so thin. At work in the castle kitchens, she fixed veil-thin crepes, angel food cake, steamed bok choy—and still the Queen wouldn't eat. Between meals, she called her kitchen sisters to order, reminded them of their long workdays and terrible wages, and taught them union songs. Sometimes she stole home a meringue and her sisters let the sweet air melt on their tongues.

The second Phoebe was an artist, her job to take photos of tourists dressed up in costumes from an earlier time: the beaded buckskins of the Indian Maiden who'd gone over the falls in a white canoe, the French aerialist's tight bathing costume, or the orange life jacket worn by little Roger when he tumbled unexpectedly from a boat—survivors all. At night she retreated to the tumble-down barn behind the farmhouse and fashioned crushing blue-black-purple sculptures out of felt, some that looked like plums and some that looked like daggers until you stepped round to the other side and realized they looked like nothing at all.

The third Phoebe took in laundry. Every day she carried huge loads of linens back and forth between the hotels and the house where a cauldron bubbled and a wringer waited to squeeze the clothes flat before she hung them to dry on the lines zigzagging like a spiderweb across the yard. At times she was so bored she thought she'd split her skin or her head would explode, but she had a good memory for which underwear belonged to which customer. As she washed and folded, she dreamed of escape, though to where or what or with whom, she didn't know.

The youngest, whom the others simply called Baby, was the sweetest and most beautiful, with big brown eyes like the star of a Japanese comic book and flowing hair like a pre-Raphaelite heroine. She loved to wear red and pink together, feathers in her hair, as many shiny baubles as possible, and when she left school, she found a calling as a fortune-teller. She took her clients' hands gently between her own and told each one something completely unexpected but true. Her sisters indulged her, letting her sleep late on her days off, washing her delicates by hand, keeping the ripest berries and saltiest almonds for her to snack on, and waiting up for her when she stayed out late, not to scold her when she returned but to help her off with her tight dancing shoes. You might think that all this spoiled Baby, but in fact the opposite was true. With each indulgence, Baby became more grateful, more tender, more loving and caring.

The castle is decorated all over with mirrors, angled every which way so that in none of them can you see your own reflection. Instead, you see someone across the street and half a block away, but because you are looking into a mirror, you expect to see yourself and so suffer many sequential moments of confusion.

One day, the third Phoebe went off into the forest—chasing a client's lacy handkerchief taken by the breeze? following a kitten (she loved cats) or a golden deer?—and the giant found her walking down a fire road, looking blankly at the white-barked birches and quaking aspens and thinking of nothing at all. He cut off her feet so that she couldn't run away, then slung her over his shoulder and took her home with him.

The deer came and told her sisters what had happened, advising them to rescue her from the magical box in which the giant had locked her. Even though the box was full of lovely glittering things, and even though in it one could not feel pain, it was not like home.

That was that, they thought. How would they ever get her back?

One by one, as I've told you, the two eldest transformed themselves into skunks and porcupines and went after him with spoons and nets, but nothing worked because the giant's wife always saved him with vats of tomato juice to remove the smell and needle-nose pliers to remove the quills and soothing salves of toothpaste and copious amounts of Vicodin. Sometimes in these stories, the giant's wife will help, tired of her monstrous husband, but not in this one.

And so it was Baby's turn.

"How is it done?" she asked her sisters, and following their directions to breathe and push and push, she turned herself into a damselfly with delicate wings and an iridescent blue abdomen, a strong flyer who could stop in midair, dart sideways, and even fly backward. She flew off and a fairy tossed her a shiny egg, which she caught in the basket of her legs and which became a pretty pink ball and then a crystal ball, although crystal ball gazing had never been her forte. In two other encounters, her tenderness served her well, and she received a needle and a poisonous flower. When she got to the giant's house, she relied on his curiosity and stupidity. Luckily he had plenty of both. "Hello," she said, and he said, "Holy cow, a talking dragonfly! Come here, wife, and look at this!" When his wife appeared, the youngest Phoebe poisoned them both and freed her sister.

The giant is their father, of course. Yes, I know this doesn't make sense. Their father, the King, lives in the castle at the center of town with his second wife, the blond witch.

When they were little, they sat in a circle with their friends and played the game The Little Bird. "Year of the bird, year of the bird," they chanted and passed around a matchbox from which a tiny heavy metal bird wrapped in red flannel might pop out at any time. Or maybe a dry leaf or a budding twig, dandelion fluff, rabbit turd, rusty bottle cap, cat's paw. "All fall, all fall," they chanted as they waited to see what would appear. These items were not magical. As soon as an item appeared, the child holding the matchbox leapt up and ran around the circle until the item took wings and flew off. If it flew to the south, that meant good weather. If it flew to the north, snow, no matter the time of year. If it flew to the east, they would find golden candies by their dinner plates that evening, and if it flew to the west, they must all scramble for home. Those times are long gone now.

I could tell you the story of how one slipped over the edge of the falls by accident. I could tell you the story of their tunneling to escape.

The youngest Phoebe enchanted the giant with the pink ball—it floated in the air and turned all sorts of colors and always returned to its owner no matter how far it was thrown. While he was playing with the ball, she placed the flower in her hair. He found her so pretty he let her come close and she stabbed him with the needle. The usual poison symptoms ensued until he staggered and died, his fall shaking the earth.

Or she steals a wasp's stinger and a scorpion's poison, or they give her these things willingly after she performs some small service for them. All the sisters are searching, but in searching, they lose each other. The giant takes only the feet, not the sister, and she's been left at home while they search (obviously—she has no feet!). She keeps calling to the others; they keep calling to each other—*Fee-bee!! Fee-bee!!* Until it drives the giant's wife crazy. The siren loves only her own song.

Or there are three princesses and three princes who rescue them, as it should be. Or only one. Or twelve. There are never four of anything but in this version there are.

In another version, they are four generations of the same family rather than sisters: Grandmother, Mother, Daughter, Granddaughter. Tzipporah, Perle, Frayda, Phoebe. All called Faigale, the little bird.

Finally one day, the giant's wife caught the youngest sister, alone in a field. "All right," she said. "All right, I'll find your sisters for you. I'll even return the feet (though I don't think they'll do your sister much good now—we've picked nearly all the meat off of them). There's one condition though—you, none of you, can be human again. You must live out your lives as birds." And so the youngest acquiesced and all the sisters came running, yes even the one with no feet, and the giant's wife turned them into birds to spend their days catching flies, and away they flew until they landed here.

Moon Child

On the night of the eclipse, Mona stood in the park planning her escape. The moon went from white to a lustrous red, so dark and swollen that she wanted to suck it down the way she did berries in summer. "Blood Moon," it was called.

"Oh, harvest moon," a neighbor warbled, a voice she could not distinguish—young from old, male from female.

She wondered where she would run to. Home was impossible now, with its closed window, caged with Mother and Father and Sister and Brother. Before, she'd run across the grass to the swings, and swing UP and OVER the bar. Now that she was older, she was imprisoned with the shirts they asked her to mend, demanding tiny stitches, and the games of double solitaire they asked her to play, demanding the cards be laid out in even rows, and the cakes they asked her to bake from gluten-free flour, egg substitute, and Stevia, and finally the frosting they asked her to mix, demanding the food coloring be added drop by tiny drop to reach the perfect shade of pink.

To be fair, she wasn't the only one working—no Cinderella, she. They all tidied up frantically, demanded these same things of each other, went to no balls. Mona was the only one who seemed to mind.

When the shadow of Earth slipped off the moon, like a silk negligee slipping off a movie star's shoulder, she laid the cards out on the grass, in a sort of skyscraper shape, not caring if they got damp. "Each card is a hotel room and I'll go to the one at the top," she thought, but Mona didn't know where that hotel was, and she let a dog trample the cards before he sat beside her, leaning his shoulder up against hers and panting.

Behind her, the neighbor still sang to the moon, and now the moon's bright light let Mona see that he—white-eyed, tattooed—was an old man in a cape. "Only one if by land but a multitude if by sea," he said and pointed to the water where her raft waited, bosomed by waves, feted by a striped awning, palatial. He stripped her. They were the only two left in the park. Her little girl breasts needed to be covered but not by the linens from home. I know you think the old guy's going to be predatory, dangerous, that she's risking too much, so young (she looks older than her twelve years), but you can't live as if each neighbor is an enemy, each family member a boss. In fact, that is a kind of death. This is what Mona told herself even as she shivered.

From his backpack, the old man pulled a fine mesh dress, impenetrable as armor and threaded with blue, pinned it to her most gently, and she knew she'd put on a magical garment with secret pockets and the ability to ward off storms.

Down the hill she walked, dog beside her shaking his toy chicken like mad in his mouth.

"Oh, the moon!" Burst through clouds. Supported. Balanced on ice and thorns.

"Now this is a beginning!"

Seventh

Once . . . No.

Twice?

Not here, but far away.

The girl—youngest of seven girls (twins and twins and twins and then her), silent but smart—stared into the closet, saw a tumble that could have been discarded chickens, nesting dogs, a cauldron of bones. Her golden hair fell over her face.

Lolly. Her name was Lolly.

Three times this happened.

A sound like the closet inhaling. And then, "Money's short," it said. "We can't feed them," it said. Someone else said, "Don't, darling. Don't. You're making me sad." And the first: "They could fend for themselves." And the other: "Wait. Maybe I'll get paid tomorrow?"

Herbs hanging from the rod emitted odors of vanilla, thyme, and sage. All that was left: ghosts of turkey and pie. A light switch operated nothing.

Lolly swished her skirts, blue with a white apron over top. She wondered if escaping her fate meant leaving home or finding some way to stay. There would be many obstacles to overcome, she thought, and helpers? Not so much. Maybe a bee. Maybe a rat or, in the park, a squirrel. Not even a rabbit—or a dog. Dogs were smart. Her sisters were useless, bopping to bubblegum pop on their iPods. She peered more deeply into the closet.

Here, in the first sphere, she chose toe shoes, that slick not-quite-pink. The pet goldfish watched her crisscross the ribbons and tie them. She'd been doing pliés and ronds de jambe from the youngest age, and had just gone up on pointe. Carefully packed lambswool protected her toes from blisters. She did a pirouette for practice, the world a winking refraction. Blood on the parquet floor, spin-art red. "Did you bleed through those shoes again?" her father would say. The other time, he'd been so mad, but the pain was nothing to him.

Out the door Lolly went, keys in one hand to lock the deadbolts, gum wrappers in the other, ones she'd been saving for the jokes. Her sisters trailed behind her, like ducks following their mother even though she was the youngest. Down the shitty hall. The smell, as always: musty, bacon, Windex. Her toe shoes clumped down the six flights of linoleum stairs. When she opened the door to the street, sound hit her, and heat—yellow taxis honking, air brakes, a boom box shouting *Saturday Night Fever*. A little rat terrier was waiting for her, a tilt to his head, inquisitive eyes, feet planted squarely. He seemed well-fed, with a firm tummy and a happy stump of a tail. Even though there were more wise cats than dogs in the old stories, she followed him. Little dogs are said to trot, or sometimes scamper, but this one did some sideways skip thing that lifted him nearly off the sidewalk. Already, so early in the morning, people crushed to work. Above, squeezed between the apartment buildings, the sky was already turning white. Air conditioners already dripped. Fans already whirred. Lovely linen suits were already crumpled and T-shirts already sweat stained. The dog turned right at the avenue and only his little tail was visible, shivering in some abbreviated Morse code. Means to keep walking, Lolly guessed. She was going, but where? When the little dog disappeared, she disappeared too. Would her sisters even notice or would they happily stand on the corner, waiting for the light to change and discussing the shirt that boy wore to the dance, knitting patterns in complex algorithms, Minecraft? And she was in a museum. Or a hotel ballroom. Or a castle. There were chandeliers: something, something, crystal, something, teardrop. You've all seen those in enough movies, perhaps with someone swinging on them. Suddenly this thought drilled her head: Wait—no money for food but money for chandeliers?

And then, she was back home. I guess, Lolly thought, that trail of crushed papers worked. It was OK for a while, family dinners where each sister told a riddle about what had happened at school before the oldest twins went off to work on their college applications. But then, too soon, again, her sisters were hungry; peanut butter and jelly sandwiches once reviled were now described lovingly, as if speaking about them would stick the peanut butter to the roofs of their mouths. Again, the closet was open. Again, she was staring down at a tumble of bones. No exhale but her own. Because she had neglected her corset, her ribs creaked. Her breasts were just needing a bra. Where were her parents? Out to rob a bank? This was the second sphere. She sat on the floor and put on her old PF Flyers that she hoped would make her speedy like they had in the old days, and told her sisters to do so too. They ventured out—again—but in this sphere, it was impossible to exit the building. Through the highest windows, she could see the East River in one direction and the Hudson in the other, the Empire State Building in one direction and the Twin Towers in the other, and far off, past them, the Statue of Liberty raised her torch. For hours, she and her sisters ranged the stairs and traversed the hallways, jiggling each doorknob. Some of the doors opened, but each time Lolly found herself back in front of the same closet. Her feet did disturb the dust, and her hands on the banisters mopped up that sticky, black, New York City combo of dirt and soot. It was like being chained but not exactly, more like caged but the girls would never fatten. The hallways were hot and silent, and her sisters had dropped and curled in separate corners. They were napping, their faces sweaty, each with a palm under her twin's cheek. One sister held a corsage; another, a thick book; a third cradled a red patent leather pump. The bee buzzed in Lolly's ear. No rest for you, Lolly, it seemed to say.

She tried to wake her sisters but they were locked in sleep, dreaming of ogres. When she opened the closet again, there was no nest; there were no shoes but there was a door. This was the third sphere. Trees grew up around her, and she saw a path that skittered and slipped downhill through fallen leaves toward a lake. Up above in the branches, a demented squirrel chattered and grinned. "Take a step," it said to her. She was in a land where squirrels were not just intelligent but verbal. Her sisters would surely laugh at her. "Verbal in ENGLISH," Lolly imagined saying. "How else do you think I knew which way to go? And what were you doing while I was gone, anyway?" This tiny amount was the most she'd said in forever. Her sisters talked to each other in their own secret languages, a different language for each set of twins. You'd think she'd understand them by now, but "Anyway," she said. When they were still kids, sitting in a circle, flicking marbles, they'd talked this way, paying her no mind. She loved the blue swirly marbles but she never won them. OK, that's the past, she told herself; she was here now, in the woods. And she was barefoot, and the path had disappeared, and somewhere her sisters were hiding—no, being kept hidden, being kept from their husbands and children, not allowed to venture out to their offices or see their patients or paint their pictures. From behind, a hand grabbed her, lifted her into the air, and flung her over a leather-clad shoulder. Upside down, her heart slid into her throat. She could choke herself or scream, it didn't really matter because she knew that here, no one existed except her and him. The hands holding her ankles were icy and tight. One step and they were at the lake, then in the lake, then over it. Head swinging, she watched the man's boot heels kick up mud. Another step, atop a mountain, and the man stopped, breathing hard. He tossed her into a cave where a car was parked, near a pile of broken bones and half-cooked flesh. Odor of roasting and rot. You know—cobwebs, bat shit, paintings of bison. She closed her eyes. When I open them, I'll be at the closet again, Lolly thought, but when she did, she wasn't. Now the man was asleep, his huge hands still grasping a rope that ended in a knot around her waist. Busily chewing at the knot was the squirrel. Lolly thought about finding the car keys, having to dig her hands deep into the man's pants. She was so far from home and she suspected she wasn't as smart as she'd thought. But then there were the man's boots: made of thigh-high burgundy leather, lined with green paisley silk, adorned with various buckles and zippers. Forget about the car, the squirrel said, and Lolly lifted her feet very high and slid them down into the boots, down the shaft and through the throat, past the counter, instep, and vamp, until she could finally stretch her toes. She rocked back and forth on the stacked heels. Then they wrapped the man in moss so cold wouldn't wake him.

Dawn. The clouds had lifted. The breeze had warmed. One step and she reached the lake. Another step and she crossed it. Another and she was back in town. And one more brought her to her old building where she found her parents sitting on the stoop, fanning themselves with takeout menus from the Chinese place down the block and arguing—again, as if she'd never left. They looked at her seven-league boots, her black jeans and the extra-large T-shirt she'd knotted at her waist, at her tangly hair and sparkly purse, and at the nine ice cream cones she was somehow managing to hold and that were somehow managing not to melt in the August evening.

"Let's go in," her parents said in unison. "Your sisters will be home any minute for the holiday."

She didn't know which holiday. She didn't know if her foot would strike concrete or if it would sink clean through the steps when she tried to enter, just as if the building were a ghost.

The Cathedral Is a Mouth

I've heard that the great Gothic cathedrals, with their arches, ribs, and vaults, were modeled after trees in the forest, the way trees reach up and their branches intertwine. We can be lying on the forest floor, pine needles infiltrating our hair; we can be staring up at the sky, a pale miasmic shifting blue that seems even further away than usual because it's on the other side of the trees; we can be lying there, staring up as the trunks etch up into the sky, and our hands can touch, our fingers intertwining just like the branches, and beyond them, in the twinkle, our eyes drawn heavenward, we can see God.

I don't believe any of this. Not the miasmic sky, not God, not even the pine needles, but there is something beautiful about cathedrals.

In Paris, a girl walks down the central aisle of Notre-Dame in her dark pleated skirt, white blouse, crested blazer, Audrey Hepburn hair, and black ballet flats, looking like someone's fantasy of a teenage schoolgirl, although teenage schoolgirls rarely dress exactly like this anymore, except ironically. She is clutching books to her chest, or a violin, or a box of buttons, and she is going to meet someone who she thinks will change her life. She is sweating a bit because she's nervous. Right now, she has a place to sleep (a corner of her school's basement) but nowhere to live. Having received a message rolled up like a scroll inside the toothbrush case she secretes in the cracked wall of her school's bathroom, she believes she has come for an audition—violinist, reciter of poems for a blind woman, babysitter, seamstress. She hopes any of these positions will come with a chambre de bonne, its tiny window looking out to miasmic sky.

Three people sit in the front row of pews: an old man hiding a tabby cat under his long coat; a one-armed widow; and a boy thinking of

28

his mother, long dead or right now dying, and playing the game *Monument Valley* on his phone. The girl allows her eyes to range over them.

If she goes with the first, she will become a tender of mice, a preparer of English trifles.

If she goes with the second, she will become a breaker of teacups, a baker of bread, feeder and fed.

For the third, she will deliver clean handkerchiefs, walk him to school, translate his silent desires. He hasn't spoken since his mother took ill. Even to Maman, he hasn't talked.

She doesn't know why anyone would need a live-in violinist but she hopes nonetheless.

Now that she's thought of them, any of these possibilities seem real. A ticking inside her—she is aware of the avenues her life might follow, but she hears no one say, "Excuse me, young lady," no one clear their throat to catch her attention as she passes, and decides she must have missed her appointment by only the few minutes she was delayed at her lesson.

She wanders through the various chapels, looking at the paintings and wondering if she should pay to light a candle in memory of her mother's soul although this is not her religion.

When she steps back on to the plaza in front of the cathedral, where the pigeons have congregated, some landing on children's heads, the autumn twilight has set in and the sky is purple behind the Eiffel Tower. She will return to the locker at Saint-Germain-des-Prés where she has stowed her things.

I've called her a girl but that's not what she calls herself. She might say she's a young lady or a young woman; she feels resilient, competent. And she is. She's got money, enough for food and violin lessons, just not enough for rent, and she actually has a place to stay—her uncle's— where there's a fold out sofa bed for her in the tiny foyer. But she hasn't been "home" for days.

When she gets to the locker, the lock has been broken. (She can't think about it, about what's been taken.) When she gets back to her school, the door has been locked. She could call her violin teacher, but they have the most distant, professional relationship (he calls her "Miss" and she calls him "Professor"), and anyway her phone is dead. So. A café bathroom. A bench in the Métro station. In each place, someone stumbles upon her, says, "Mon Dieu!" and she scurries away. Finally, back to the cathedral but even there the door is locked at night. Instead, she shivers by the sandbox between the building and the river where a man emerges from his nest of blankets and cats, all suddenly mewling, and then stands aside, inviting her to take his place under them. Don't tell me she's stupid for going in. She played in that sandbox as a child. He is her father's age or her uncle's—she supposes—but looks nothing like her uncle or like the father she remembers. His hand on her thigh is appalling but when she runs, he doesn't follow her, again unlike her uncle. At least she knows where her mother is, buried in Montparnasse, against her wishes, with her forbearers, some illustrious rabbis. But a cemetery at night? She believes those gates would be locked too.

She walks. Her shoes will last. The next day is Saturday. Back in the cathedral, yet again—*why?* Something pulls her. She sees an old woman, the widow, worrying beads. "J'ai froid," the girl thinks and the woman opens her arm wide and the girl shrinks to pocket-size, the size of a book, and slips inside the woman's black shawl to hear her mumbling. "You don't belong here. I will take you away." It's dark under the wool, but then it's dark in the cathedral anyway, barely a splash of color on the floor through the rose window, the stones soot-blackened from all those candles. She remembers the female figures of Ecclesia and Synagoga on either side of the central portal, the second woman with the tablets of the Ten Commandments broken at her feet. Is that what they still think of Jews? The statue has a serpent coiled around her eyes, too, and the girl vaguely remembers:

- Therefore shall ye lay up these my words in your heart and in your soul, and bind them for a sign upon your hand, that they may be frontlets between your eyes.
- And ye shall teach them to your children, speaking of them when thou sittest in thine house, and when thou walkest by the way, when thou liest down, and when thou risest up.

from High Holy Days, the only time she ever went to synagogue. Before her grandparents were deported, sent from one camp to another and then finally to Auschwitz, they stripped the mezuzah from their door frame, put it in her mother's hand, and closed her fist around it. Then they sent her away to a children's home in southern France run by the Oeuvre de Secours aux Enfants. When her mother moved back to Paris, an adult, she tacked the mezuzah to a new doorframe, slanted inward as if inviting God to enter. Like three-quarters of the adults in Israel, her mother had wanted to believe that it guarded her home, to believe it repelled a divine anger in which she didn't believe. She knew the force to repel was human.

Inside the book is a book. Inside the mezuzah case is the parchment klaf, on which has been scribed, with special ink, God's instructions for affixing the mezuzah, the words from Deuteronomy: "And thou shalt write them upon the doorposts of thine house, and upon thy gates." A reminder of a reminder of a reminder.

(clean underwear, a scarf and matching mittens, sheet music—Bach Partitas and Mozart Sonatas, fountain pen and ink, school books, winter boots)

They are moving now, and the girl hears voices, the tinkling bell of a door opening, the smell of butter and sugar. "Here," the old woman says, and slips a baguette under her shawl. "You need to eat." Her one hand pulls bits of bread, finds the girl's lips, and shoves the bread in. When they come out of the bakery, the girl no longer smells diesel or hears engines. In the book inside the book inside the shawl, she smells rain on cobbles, smells horse. It's Saturday; she hears a match struck by a Shabbas goy. They're wandering through the old Marais, past the precursors of Sacha Finkelstein's with its pain de seigle and the precursors of the popular falafel joints along the Rue des Rosiers (Le Roi, L'As, Chez H'Annah). In the gutter, next to the rag that guides the rainwater down the drain, she finds her mother's favorite ring, a tiny ruby surrounded by even tinier pearls. I've called her a girl, and this is most definitely what she is when she finds the ring and starts crying: a girl, a daughter, wetting the old woman's shawl. She has left things at her uncle's. When he's at work, she'll go back there to retrieve them, stuff them into her old satchel, and never trust those lockers again.

But now she needs a nap. She feels a gentle hand set her down. "I'm going," the old woman says. It's gotten dark, chilly on the bench where she's been left. She hears the rancid music of a carousel spinning in the middle of Place de la République, a double-decker of animals and chariots and flashing lights and children's screeches of delight. Her father(?) brought her here once, she thinks. If she pays a sous, she might have a place to sleep for the night, lullabied, circled around and circling. Her uncle's place isn't far away but her pages have turned. That volume is finished.

(ring, ticket stub from an Itzak Perlman concert, blanket, pebbles for the grave)

In the café below her uncle's apartment, there's a pinball machine. She used to spend hours with it herself, but this morning, Sunday, a boy is playing when she goes in for une noisette. From the counter (the coffee cheaper there) she watches his big backpack slide down his back, his whole body rock side to side. Bells he doesn't seem to hear. Then he shrugs: lost again, she thinks. Those could be her own younger shoulders shrugging.

When his game is done and he has no more money for tokens, the boy slips out, and the barman looks at her and then the door. It's time to go too. Where—in the rain? The synagogue: no one will be there. A window on the side? In the back? Some way in? but the door is unlocked and people are there, a boy (a different boy—she checks) and his tutor, preparing. She sits down to watch them. Although he nods his head and follows along the words in the Torah, pointing with the yad, he's silent. How will he intone the prayers, and especially, how will he make his bar mitzvah speech?

Once the boy is gone, the man comes over to her. "Are you a Jew?" he asks.

"Oui, je suis juive."

"Have you been bat mitzvahed? It's never too late," he says, leaning toward her, proffering a book, but she puts her hand up.

"No," she says, "for that you have to believe." When he shrugs and turns away, she thinks, well, that's a lot of shrugging today.

"I'll be locking up soon," he says. Before going out, he turns back. "The synagogue isn't necessary," he says, "just a minion."

She hides under a bench. She'll stay there tonight. Tomorrow, Monday, she can go to her uncle's while he's at work. There she can eat, take some more of her things. Her bankbook—she really needs that, and her passport, just in case. Some extra clothes. In her pocket, she finds hard candy, croissant crumbs.

When she wakes, the boy is there, finger to his lips. Under one arm is a book; under the other, his phone, which starts playing some soothing music. He has teffilin tied to his head, his upper arm. He wraps his prayer shawl around her, but he also drags her out the door into the night, shaking his head.

(skin cells, bile, scrap of letter on which there is half of her father's signature)

When she had to leave her uncle's, she thought she had three wishes left, but really she had nothing. Except that she was still alive. She could feel her heart beating, she could feel the breath in her body and see it outside her body, billowing into the night air.

(inhale, exhale—whose?)

She is hungry, she is wet, and the key to her uncle's door will not turn, but she sits inside the cathedral of her own mouth—restored, refurbished, the walls painted white, faux marble that the traditionalists hate, black Madonna now white—and looks out between her own teeth. A sound reverberates, arching up to the ribs of her palate. Others are in here, screeching or heckling, or are they singing with her. Is that her own voice she hears? She remembers being told to pray what's in her heart, to say the words in her own way. This is all that's left, all that she can hold on to: breath like a bow across her strings.

Return of the Media Five

I am this heart, this brain, only these, right now—no other. This is what Susan (that's her name now) tells herself every morning upon waking. She opens her eyes and sees the flaking ceiling above her, sees the wash of sunlight coming through leaves. She touches her chest, feels her heart beating steadily—no rush of fear—and exhales. She's alone. She touches her head, hair just starting to gray and she's not bothering to color it. This can be my new disguise, she thinks, my new self. One of the million selves she's been in the last twenty-odd years. She rubs her eyes and before she can silence herself again, she remembers days when she thought more, remembered more: a million legs all running toward the Pentagon or induction center or federal courthouse. A Viet Cong flag. Giant puppets of Kissinger, Nixon, McNamara. Or their heads atop the bodies of gigantic hawks, perched among the blackened trees of a burned landscape. Bring the war home. A placard of a napalmed child. If people see, they will join us and this atrocity will have to stop. A million hands waving. A million arms, fists raised in salute. They were the million legs and hands of her—her legs and hands—the million-limbed body of resistance, then revolution. Why does she allow these things to come back to her today? Because it's spring and her curtains are the color of a daffodil she handed to a child once at a demonstration? She remembers when the remembered voices were always with her, singing off-key but loudly together. She never felt alone. But then suddenly she was alone, amputated from everyone and everything she knew. Most mornings she silences these memories of memories, she manages to.

It's a matter of self-preservation: if she does not remember her past, she'll make no slips, allow no one to find her, avoid the harsh slap of the

34

law in the person of a policeman's hand. For they still behave that way, they do. When she sees it on TV, she must remind herself she looks like—no, *is*—a harmless, middle-aged white lady, no Rodney King. Her arresting officer would be younger than she is, wouldn't remember the 1960s, wouldn't even have been *born* then. She rises, washes her face—most mornings—and with the night's sleep puts aside, again, the actions and the years on the run and all the melodrama. "Oh, not a million. Don't be ridiculous," she says aloud. She's taken on only a dozen or so personas in all these years: despite the plethora of glossy boxes, hair dye actually comes in only so many colors. Days, she goes on with baking or laundry or typing or childcare or waitressing or whatever other ho-hum job she's doing, goes on with taking the bus to work and stopping in the grocery store on the way home, goes on with a movie on the weekends, goes on with volunteering at the homeless shelter, goes on with answering when her newest friend uses her newest name. She goes on with showing her fake ID and paying in cash (she used checks for a while but was always scared she'd sign her real name), goes on with moving or staying put as long as she can keep her stories from contradicting each other, as long as no one comes up to her in a bar and says, "Don't I know you from somewhere?" even when that's probably just a pickup line, moves on to the next in a string of casual affairs or one-night stands. Sometimes she reminds herself that she could end this, contact a lawyer, retake her real name and her past. The charges, if any, have surely been dropped. Someone could find out for her. Even Bernardine Dohrn and Bill Ayers resurfaced long ago—look at the lives they've made for themselves. But then she thinks, What for? She's even been able to testify in front of the legislature, an advocate for the homeless gals in the shelter, with her fake name. Her past is so surely and totally past, the people from her past like puppets with no hands to guide them, the places of her past inhabited by new occupants. She's landed here, two towns over from the Connecticut town she grew up in, but the landscape has been so utterly changed by bulldozers, subdivisions, Pierre Deux fabrics, strip malls, insurance brokers, real estate agents, and private beaches that she barely recognizes it. Well, so it goes. And the self of that past? Despite this morning's rememberings . . . would she recognize her?

She rises, pulls on her robe, examines her teeth in the mirror—a totally ordinary morning. Her room opens directly onto the landing at the top of the stairs. Downstairs, she shares the living room and kitchen with the other inhabitants of this no-name boarding house, a dry counterpart to true communal living. Here the inhabitants ignore each other, clean the kitchen and bath of all traces of themselves every day, no crusts of whole wheat bread sticky with peanut butter on the counters, no long hairs winding themselves down the bathtub drain. The other bedroom doors are locked, everyone either still asleep or gone—she can never keep track of her ever-changing housemates' patterns. In the kitchen, the air smells of exhaust, dust, pollen. Unlike the window in her bedroom, stuck since the year's first warm day, this one opens. Outside, the leaves have only just unfolded on the trees but it's already hot and humid. Your typical East Coast leap across spring, Susan thinks. She remembers spring elsewhere: the chilly Seattle stretch from February to June, the heavy Southern odor of magnolia, rain swept across a Paris street, the month of heat in northern California before the fog settled in, yellow crocuses in the Midwest and the smell of mud, a blanket of rotten snow beneath pine trees at the edge of Penobscot Bay, cactus flowers.

Unusual, someone's left a mess of the newspaper on the dining table, and she straightens the pages while she waits for her toast to brown, seeks the front page with her usual mix of curiosity and trepidation. It happens often enough—the reappearance of a fugitive on their way to an arraignment—that she feels vindicated in having these emotions. Really, though, why should she feel trepidation? Just because A and B got themselves arrested doesn't mean she's next. She remembers the day she found them smiling up at her from the front page, older certainly, still flashing the peace sign. And had that been X's face in the background, a profile she thought she recognized, turned in conversation with a cop. Not an image she wants to pursue. Today she doesn't find a face or name to recognize. She scans the stories with scant interest, glances at the date—May 3. May 3 already? she thinks languidly. Then more sharply: May 3 *already*. Her period must be at least two weeks late. It can't be, she thinks, she can't have managed—maybe, somehow—after all these years, to get herself knocked up. She recalculates dates, remembers bleeding just as the crocuses bloomed, remembers looking at the muted purple of the flower one minute and a few minutes later at the petals of blood on her underpants. Surely she has to have bled since.

She pushes her chair back from the table and places her hand on her belly. She has felt bloated for a while—since when?—and remembers a strange episode of tummy rumblings and poppings she'd never experienced before. There's no denying her period is late. Maybe she's premenopausal? No, surely too young for that. So—pregnant? Really? At forty-two, isn't she too old for that and all it leads to? Diapers and noise, her own place and a lease in her own name, chasing a naked toddler as he runs through the park gates and then, patiently, turning him from an animal into a human being—she's seen friends try. A wave of nausea hits her, but she knows it's fear, she *knows* it's fear. Surely she recognizes her body's response to fear after all this time. Once, she thought she'd marry and have two-point-five perfect children, time for four years of career first. Then she thought she'd marry—some hokey ceremony in a backyard with flowers in her hair instead of a veil—but have no children, she and X so committed to the Movement there'd be no time for children and their lives too dangerous for children to join anyway. Then she expected she'd never marry but still produce a brood of children, all living in some communal paradise. The past dozen years or so, she hasn't thought about having children at all. And now what? What has she done? If it's real, what will she do? Terminate? Pass the child along to someone else? Have the child? But she'd have to tell him something about her past: events and ramblings, fear, loneliness and its antidotes, slivers of joy. Some people pass along photographs or spoon collections, one tiny teaspoon for every city they've lived in, or the tattered remnants of relatives' clothes, or jewelry, or hand-stitched quilts, but she would need to find other residues to explain.

∾

Skokie, Illinois—when they first ran, and she joined up with X. Where? It was night. The house of friends of friends of Movement friends. The bed, an ancient iron thing painted white in a dingy room.

But surprisingly, the mattress was wonderful, one of those tufted hotel affairs, the sort of thing she remembered sleeping on as a teenager on a family trip to some wedding or funeral. She'd slept very well there.

Bangor, Maine—her room behind the health food store, a place filled with dusty bins of whole wheat flour and the sour smell of almond butter left clinging to the lip of the self-grind machine, a roaming dog, wilted sunflowers, and her coworkers, these few leftover hippies, filtering summer sunlight through half-closed lids. They sold the grains and produce mostly to each other, the rest of the population having abandoned the hot downtown for the mall out near the airport, with its air-conditioned supermarket, discount clothing store, and giant five-and-dime.

Tallahassee, Florida—the shape of a man's back—ridiculous to think she couldn't remember more than that—curved as the bowl of a wooden spoon and the dusky luscious color, too, of worn wood.

Wisconsin—snow outside the window, the white of apocalypse.

San Francisco—her room in the Haight after its heyday, the detritus of a thousand marijuana nights. The very walls infused with the fusty smell, a Day-Glo rainbow painted on an indigo background, rolled-up black light posters someone had left behind, a mattress on the floor, and a sink in the corner. By then she'd stopped smoking weed herself, finding even one toke gave her a headache. From the bay window, she saw the house across the street with its peeling gray paint, a palm tree, a madrona's smooth red skin. She's heard new owners have since repainted the houses in bright colors, colors visitors think inspired the Summer of Love but it's not true. She remembers empty, fog-filled days after she and X finally split up (despite everything, she still doesn't allow herself to think his names—his real name, his nicknames, or even his aliases—for fear she'll slip and he'll get caught), walking around in a daze, damp and cold in July, pulling on sweaters she found in trash cans. She shaded her eyes against the midday glare when the sun threatened to burn through the fog, gathered her skirt around her legs, slipped her hand into a pocket and brought out the only thing she'd taken of his, a leather key fob darkened with the oil from his hands. Until this point, she kept the past with her. She'd been calling herself Heather for nearly two years, but if someone said "Betsy" on the bus, she still needed to stop herself from turning around. After this she let the past—her name, her memories of her family, her desires, her dreams, her beliefs—drift away.

Seattle—Lucy married Richard. He thought she was a local girl, and actually she *had* lived in the city longer than he. He'd come straight from college, worked for Boeing. They married and she spent years in the rain, waiting to have the baby he thought would make their lives complete. She grew flowers in their backyard, learning which perennials liked wet and dark, thrived on only two months of sun. In June and September her garden was riotous. They made love in the bedroom overlooking it, and she was sure there'd be a baby. Then October would come, and November, and the sky would lower and she'd bleed.

The commune in New Mexico—was that before or after Seattle? She's not sure of any of this chronology. She remembers fleeing rain, fleeing Richard's disappointment and anger, but not necessarily to the commune. Goodness, that must have been the late '70s already, maybe later. The commune with its few low-slung adobe buildings, its teepee of pine logs the men had dragged down from the nearest mountain, its vegetable fields scratched into inhospitable soil, must have been gone by then—along with its barefoot children sharing books, its men with glorious, matted hair, its women kneading bread dough and trying to bake in a wood-fired oven. She'd loved the smell of yeast, the brown dough forming a thin skin that dried on her fingers and the heels of her hands. Or perhaps she's remembering images from *Easy Rider*, rather than her own life. Perhaps her escape from rain and Richard was into a movie theater just across town where they were already showing a retrospective of movies about the '60s. She can't trust her own judgement. But she remembers Buddy Sunflower, the little boy who ran along the top rail of the fence in his bare feet, absconded with hammer and nails and pieces of scrap wood. He'd pull her by the hand, show her stuff he'd made: This is an airplane, this is a spaceship, this is a robot, this is a conveyer belt, this is a car and a truck and a tractor. His mind was of a decidedly mechanical bent and he learned to help the men work on the real trucks by the time he was five. They used his small hands to reach in and do jobs they'd have to take the engine apart for otherwise, and he'd return to the house gleefully covered with grease. When they visited friends with a TV, he took it apart and had it figured out and back together again by the time the visit was over; he'd never even seen one before. "I'm going to be an engineer," he said proudly to anyone and everyone, but the grown-ups pooh-poohed him. "An engineer, Buddy?" they said. "They build bombers and oil refineries, they help destroy things," but he said, "Yeah, airplanes, whooooosh," and he soared his homemade wooden plane into the air. In the evening, they sometimes sat around the kitchen table and played music, songs of their own making or "Sugaree" or "This Land is Your Land . . ." Buddy climbed up into his mother's lap, laid his head against her shoulder, and took a toke of the joint every time it went around, until his glazed eyes just closed and he was carried up to bed. You could see the dirty bottoms of his feet. She'd teased him about that mechanical obsession, but he'd been her favorite, more than the little girls who ran around naked with only feathers in their hair and got tanned brown as adobe clay; more than the blond baby who always had a runny nose and whose mother kept him clean no matter what. Even now she wondered how a boy raised without electricity becomes obsessed with planes and turbines and trains and bridges, wondered where he was, the little boy who got high every night to fall asleep.

Denver, Colorado—typewriters. Officially she hadn't lived in the secretarial pool, but she didn't remember where she had slept or taken her meals. She remembered cheese sandwiches for lunch and the rows of desks, each facing away from the door and windows, to minimize distractions. Twenty heads turned every time the door opened. It would have been more efficient if their desks had faced the door. There was a busy clackety-clack in the room, the steady staccato sound of two hundred fingers hitting the keys. Other places she worked, the sound was less distinct, and she thinks perhaps that was because of the altitude, a mile in the air.

The backyard of her parent's house—tripping on mescaline. She lay on her back under a tree in its full summer dress. Gold outlined each leaf in some fusion of sun and drug. Her eyes had stitched the leaves with that golden thread. And she knew her friends were seeing things the same way. That for them, too, the achingly blue sky behind the green leaves wasn't really behind the leaves. It and the leaves and she and her friends were all part of the same fabric. Every once in a while, a startlingly white cloud would pass through her range of vision and she knew this was the physical manifestation of someone else's thought, the way each particle of air—the cool breeze and the warm sun—and the tip of each blade of grass beneath her were part of some giant thought. But who was thinking it? Stereo speakers in the windows, "Sweet Judy Blue Eyes" blasting. She remembers her mother calling from an upstairs window, "Betsy, Betsy, turn that music down!" and so this must have been before she disappeared, even before the events that made her run away, even before she joined SDS and sat through that long dark student strike at Columbia her first year there. And that girl who loved billowing dresses in paisley prints, singing, laying her head on a friend's shoulder for no matter what, rhubarb pie and pot brownies and vanilla ice cream, is just as strange to her as any of the other selves she's been.

Daffodils—their yellowness so pure, a funnel of yellow, with a ruffle at the edge. She's lived in them too.

Telluride—the summer she saw policemen on every street corner and thought they'd arrest her for looking at the sky. She'd heard that happened to some guy in Aspen, arrested for staring up at the sky. "It's just so blue, man," he'd told the cop. Marcia had the whole A-frame house to herself, and her only responsibility was taking care of a Siamese cat named Shingles. She lived in the basement, though, in a small room next to the hot water heater. She dragged down a mattress, a straightback chair, a desk lamp, stapled a dark blue sheet over the window, and only went upstairs after dark. When the guy she was seeing at the time came to visit her, she somehow, without giving away the reasons for her paranoia, convinced him to drive up the long dirt road at night and then back down it again with his lights off. She convinced him he could see by moonlight or even just starlight. "The stars, they're great, man," she told him. "You can't see them when your lights are on. You need to go in the dark, to let your eyes adjust away from the fake city light and get used to nature again." And then she left Telluride mid-week. The owners were scheduled to be back Friday anyhow, and she left enough food and water for the cat, and she didn't tell anyone where she was going. Or rather she left a vague note that provided enough information to keep people from worrying without supplying any specifics. She'd become adept at those notes by then—oh, this must have been the mid-1970s already. Or maybe it was the '80s—because in her mind, everything is the mid-1970s until suddenly it's 1990 and she's settled here and then it's two years later and it's now, 1992. She knows that her life has not just been clusters of activity punctuated by periods of hibernation, but it seems that her memories are either tinged with dying communes and the background flash of disco lights or with the sad aftermath of lots of money made and lost, moods she picked up along with discarded newspapers in bus stations. She'd read enough to know what was going on around her. And now the newspaper got delivered every morning, and there was Clinton, the hope for Clinton, whose fucking around might cost him the presidency. When was the last time she'd had some hope? Or was it desperation?

ABC, New Jersey—early 1971, she and X had posed as newlyweds and rented an immaculate suburban ranch house within striking distance of Philly and its Media suburb, complete with new shag carpeting and olive-colored appliances. X had cut his hair shorter, grown modest sideburns, wore "love beads" to parties—an affectation they laughed and laughed at. They were already ex-hippies, Movement people playing straight people who occasionally tried on the costumes of hippies. She'd parted her hair on the side and brushed it shiny, wore square-heeled pumps and suede miniskirts (not too short) with wide belts. They looked just cool enough, a cool young couple retreating from the city to maybe think about starting a family. They explained away the others: a brother just out of college, a sister between jobs, a cousin on his way back from the Peace Corps. They felt they were taking a risk with that last one but how else to explain his duffel bag, knowledge of Swahili, love of African music. They made sure to play music softly, to drive neither in nor out of their driveway at odd hours, to bring in the requisite groceries in brown paper bags from the supermarket—bags of chips, dripping packages of chicken legs, containers of coleslaw and potato salad in the same tart, creamy dressing—to keep the lawn mowed and the hedges trimmed. Betsy—she was still Betsy then—worked in a doctor's office, answering phones, filing away patients' charts. Always the first to arrive, she had a key to the office and easy access to a copy machine.

One day she came home, and the house was quiet, X and the others asleep in their clothes in midafternoon. They'd been away all night. She didn't ask where, something in the works but better for her not to know the details. She had to remain beyond reproach: "Look, man, could we ever do anything bad around *her?*" With her sweet good looks, smooth cheeks, touch of pale pink lipstick. She walked down the stairs to the basement, stripping off her work costume, ready to add it to the load of laundry she was planning, when she saw the cardboard boxes and, opening them, the files. X found her sitting on the concrete floor, in her bra and the nude-colored pantyhose she hated, oblivious to the cold. "Look what you got," she said. "Jesus, look what you got." He pretended to listen to her suggestions for hiding the boxes, for a place to move to next, but he never followed any of them. He leaned back on the couch, booted foot crossed over his other knee, tattered jeans he wore when the drapes where closed, touching his sideburns, running his hands through the thick brown hair already growing out from the straight boy's haircut. He nodded but he said, "No, that part's my job. Yours is to copy them. Just copy them and bring them back."

"What are we going to do with them?" she asked, but he deflected her with sex, easily, with all the excitement of *this*. She was turned on all the time, even at work, while she talked to some patient asking for test results, and at the same time thought about the files she'd stayed up late reading. Not exactly what they'd been looking for but even better. Jesus Christ, maybe they could bring down the whole FBI, J. Edgar Fucking Hoover too.

After dinner they brought the boxes upstairs. She was in the inner circle now, sitting on the living room floor with them, passing around the bottle of wine, passing around the files. She'd read too much to be kept in the dark. "Is this what we were looking for?" she asked as the others whooped and hollered. "I thought we were looking for stuff about the Harrisburg Six."

"We got that, we got that," someone said.

The Harrisburg Six had been accused of planning to kidnap Kissinger. What if they'd really been able to do it? That frog! No! That turtle! No! A toad, a toad! But of course Berrigan and the others weren't really going to kidnap Kissinger or blow up the heating systems in government buildings—why heating systems of all things? Only the government itself would make up such crazy things, then concoct a case to prove it. But no, not this time. They'd stolen the government's case, and the defense could be prepared.

On the other side of the room, another conversation: Hey, if we get caught, we'll be the Media Five. And a laugh. But we won't, not ever. Not even an alarm system, only in there for an hour. She doesn't remember who said what.

"Look at this," someone else said. "They spied on a congressman's daughter, notes on every fucking march she went to!"

In the files. Oh my god. Look what we've found—just what we knew all along. They're watching everyone and writing it all down—every trip to Cuba, every request for a visa to Moscow, every march—peaceful or not, every draft card burned, every bra burned, had its own photo and memo. We've got them. Jesus Christ we've got them. Listen to this, listen to this, someone said, read choice bits out loud.

That spring, she would come home from work, find the curtains drawn, yesterday's coffee cups filled with cigarette butts, that morning's dishes on the floor, papers spread everywhere, and an argument going on about whether to classify a bank robbery by a black militant group with robberies or political surveillance, whether to include draft resisters in political surveillance or create a separate category, because their final release of documents was to include a summary of all the papers they'd recovered—no one said "stolen," because a full 40 percent of the documents, the largest category, related to political surveillance, and only two of those concerned right-wing groups while all the others, over two hundred, concerned groups on the left. The other documents: mostly manuals, and then a smattering of murders, draft resisters, bank robberies, and organized crime. She'd hand over the docs she'd copied that day, to one hand or another, pick up dishes and wash them, cook dinner, usually able to rope someone in to help her.

And yes, she's not allowing herself to use names and yes that means they're all becoming one person again, which they did successfully that spring as they mailed documents to senators and all the newspapers, "serials" they called them, just like the Agency did, and wrote letters to peace activists and reporters and even the FBI itself, signed them "The Citizens' Committee to Investigate the FBI." After working their day jobs, they'd come home and work that other job, reading and sorting and analyzing documents, until they all, except her, gave up their day jobs. Then they'd all end up in one bed or another, or some of them in one bed and others wound together in another. That was that living room, that bedroom, until she came back one day two months later and saw that all the boxes were gone, and then that X and A—the other woman, deceitful diva she'd called "sister," with her guitar and her Odetta songs—were gone too. Just the other guys were left and they wouldn't say a word, busy packing up their leathers and bottle openers and pipes, and asking her would she please contact the real estate person and let him know they had to move out, handle cleaning up the place and getting their deposit back because she was the only one who could do that, the only one who was straight-looking enough, and then they walked out the door and gave her some P.O. box to send the deposit money to when it came and please send cash, they said. You'll want to use cash from now on too. And of course she did because, by god, they'd bring down the whole fucking FBI with this information. And looking back on it, they very nearly did. Hoover canceled COIN-TELPRO that spring.

So she hung tight until the lease on the house was up, told the neighbors her husband had been transferred, but three guys in suits came into the office one day and asked to speak to her privately in the doctor's consulting room. They called her "Miss" even though she had that gold band on her finger. She played up to it. When they asked her what type of copying machine they had in the office, she said she didn't know and fluttered her eyelashes. "Oh, I can never remember things like that," she said. "Sometimes I can hardly remember which buttons to push." She giggled. She knew damn well what machine it was, and she'd watched the Xerox technician fix it enough times to know how its innards worked too.

Then they asked about G. Could she tell them his whereabouts? "I really don't know," she said. "He just needed a place to stay when he came back from Africa. He was in the Peace Corps, you know."

"He was never in the Peace Corps," they said. "And I think you know that."

She chose to ignore the last remark. "Oh dear," she said. "Oh dear. You just can't trust anyone, can you?" Eventually he'd been caught, plucked from a drum circle on Sproul Plaza in Berkeley, just when she was starting to relax. Funny how she and X are the only ones left out here . . .

The men kept asking about G and A and B and X, and as she deflected and deflected, she wondered when they would ask about her own membership in SDS—a lapsed membership she reminded them when they finally did. She kept her cool. The SDS was all behind her now. It was so passé, wasn't it? She was married and working and hoping to start a family. She knew she didn't need to worry about X: he was clean. He'd never officially belonged to anything. Sweet boy, reluctant revolutionary—at least when they started, before he started saying, "We're a collective. Our lives need to be exemplary." And she, she could play the part of the reformed flower child for the FBI, for her parents, for as long as it took for them to lay off, until she could call the payphone set aside for Monday mornings at ten, and hear his voice again, hear him say he'd gotten his shit together and left the diva and now she could join him. When they asked where her "husband" (they leaned into that word with insinuation) was, she insisted that he'd been sent to Louisville and gave them the address and phone number of a Holiday Inn. The insinuation funny because he was, in fact, her husband—she had the certificate to prove it. "Oh no, Ma'am, he's not there," they said. "And I think you know that."

"Oh dear, oh no, not . . . ," she said, collapsing in a paroxysm of overlapping real and fake tears, and just wouldn't stop weeping.

"So you suspected . . ."

"Yes," she interrupted, "that gal at his office. Can you find him for me?" And she kept weeping, not because he was really supposed to be in Louisville but because she knew that one day, one day soon probably, she would not be able to find him.

∾

Now, when she emerges from the drugstore on her way to work, the pregnancy test inside a white paper bag, she allows herself to remember those moments of triumph and fear for the first time in a long, long time. Two blocks later she enters a department store. Once a splendid palace of consumerism, it's seen better days. The ladies' room is still magnificent however, its private stalls each equipped with a wash basin set into a marble counter, and she heads right there. Up the escalator, close the door, down come her jeans and underpants. With trepidation, excitement, hope, she pees onto the plastic test strip, and in the ensuing three minutes of waiting, she thinks these things:

other rooms, lost locations, reduced histories, the room where she was hit by a man, the room where she first hit a man, the room where she wept for her mother's death and later wept because she could not go to the funeral and still later wept because forever she'd be the ungrateful daughter, the room where she washed lingerie, the room where she washed lettuce and spun it in a basket so that water droplets splattered the walls, the room where she got socked in the eye by love, the room where sunlight became solid, the room that reverberated with the sound of rain, the room where the wind nestled in the corners and then struggled to get out again, the room where she made friends, the room where she said goodbye to old friends, the room where roaches armied up and down the walls all night, the room where butterflies loved her, the room where her cat gave birth, the room she'd painted yellow, the other room she'd painted green, the room long ago she'd painted purple not realizing what that dark color would do to her mood, the rooms of forgiveness and blame, of pity and rage, of calm breathing and horror, nightmare rooms and fantasy rooms, the rooms of desire and fear.

When the blue line appears, Betsy knows her son (already she's sure it will be a boy) will need to know all of them. If X reappeared, found her out . . . No, she'll need to set the wheels in motion for reemergence into her own life on her own.

The Other Road

The spring rain was delicious, although he wondered how that term might apply to something he couldn't taste. It washed lilac through the open bedroom window, the bush outside thick with flowers, and this must be what woke him from a dream of lying beside his wife, a dream he had while lying beside his wife. She had walked through the open window carrying the baby and a basket of lilacs just as he set the chime on a new clock.

In a different part of the country, his grandmother had raised him single-handedly in a cottage smelling of damp tweed and licorice. He'd been put on the train with just a basket of provisions, and he had one vague memory of the time before coming to live with her, a memory so inconsequential that I shall not relate it here.

Outside his grandmother's gate, the road had turned right to the village and left to the forest. He was allowed to walk to school in the village and he was allowed to venture in the other direction, but not as far as the forest or lake. One day, as he walked along, he glanced across the fields and for the first time, saw another road running parallel to his own. Where had it been until that day? On the other road, walked another boy, also wearing a red flannel shirt, also carrying a basket from which, even at this great distance, the smell of cookies seemed to drift. When the boys saw each other, they waved, in exactly the same way. When one stopped waving, the other did too. When the boy turned his head, he saw that the roads converged in the distance and he started to run, toward that convergence. Behind the other boy had been the shadows of a man and a woman. He ran faster and harder than ever, and when he finally stopped, he found himself at the very edge of the forest, where he sat down on a log and allowed the trees to shade him. The lake glittered below. Something about a drowning bothered him. The other boy—where had he gone? And the other road?

Soon, an old woman—not his grandmother—emerged from the forest, carrying a basket, and asked, "Are you lost?" At first the boy was relieved, but then she walked on without waiting for an answer. As he tried not to cry, a hunter emerged from the forest, his rifle over one shoulder and a sack over the other. Whistling, he passed the boy by. The boy thought of a story his grandmother had told him about a hunter returning home after a long trip, entering his house through the great front window, and joining his family. Then the boy dried his eyes on his shirt, and a woodsman emerged from the forest, his axe over one shoulder and a sack over the other. He sat down next to the boy and wiped his forehead. Something red bulged from the sack, and a familiar odor emerged, something like wolf, blood, or cookie. After a while, the woodsman told him a story about returning home after a journey, such a long journey that his mother and father have given him up for dead. He approached his home at night, watched his parents a long time through the great front window, their faces happy in the candlelight, and turned away again.

Painting Time

Your painting time and her painting time coincide, your studios side by side in the garage. At your wedding, you joked that you had his 'n' hers studios instead of his 'n' hers towels. Then afterward, after painting: dinner, dishes, TV, sex, sleep. You're both in art school and sometimes one of you leaves the house in the afternoon to attend a class. Sometimes you leave together for the grocery store or to meet friends in a bar.

After graduation, you teach drawing to community college students and clay slamming to kids at the YMCA; she works in an office part-time, just enough hours to get benefits for both of you. But eventually you feel that things need to change. You say, "I don't know how much longer I can do this, spend half the day driving around from one adjunct position to another, with my office in the trunk of the car." You paint harder, late into the night, you and she, while a different popular song blares from the radio every three minutes and the fluorescent studio lights turn your skin green. You both paint harder, but you get shown first—a group show in a co-op gallery, a solo show in a real gallery. This means you can land a full-time teaching job, and you move together to a new town, a new house, and a new garage turned into studios. Now that you're bringing in the benefits, she starts teaching part-time because offices make her crazy. And things go on like this for a while: your painting time, your teaching time; her painting time is sometimes in the car, drawing time really, stuck in traffic, driving from one adjunct position to another. On the way home from school one day, you buy her a little notebook she can clip to the sun visor of her car and the very best colored pencils so that she can even draw upside down. Sometimes she stops at the grocery store on the way home, sometimes you do. Sometimes, less often now, you go out in the evening together to meet your new friends in a bar.

The new friends have children, but it's a long time before you and she want to have children. "When will we paint?" you both say. Then, later, she starts joking about her biological clock and you start joking about your need for someone to take care of you in your old age. Beneath the joking though, you both feel a completely irrational pull, outside time and space, to become parents. Eventually you say, "Well, we'll find the time," and she says, "The baby will have to nap sometime." And so you have children: one, two, three in quick succession. She's so exhausted that she stops painting completely, and you don't fare much better. When the babies cry at night, you bring them to her for nursing. Then you lie awake, listening to the quiet sucking noises they make, thinking how you're wasting precious painting time, but you're so tired you can't imagine getting out of this warm bed and going into your cold studio. You fall back asleep, and the next time you wake up, close to dawn, you see her, propped high on pillows, still loosely holding a baby. She's sleeping sitting up. Sometimes you think of suggesting bottle feeding: she'd have more time away from the babies, time to sleep or paint; you'd have more time with them. But you never do it and wonder if that's because you believe she wants to nurse them—even at midnight—or because you don't want to give up whatever painting time you have.

Once the babies are older, you return to painting more routinely. Lucky for you the babies are late risers and you can paint for an hour before they wake, before you have to teach and attend meetings and counsel students who themselves are trying to figure out how to be painters. Sometimes, yes, you suspect your children are nocturnal animals, flying around the house like bats or crawling under the couch like porcupines. After a night like that, you're too tired to paint much, but you have always been good at using the tiniest bits of time. You can go into the studio for half an hour, fifteen minutes even, and leave behind a canvas covered with new paint.

She, on the other hand, has always been a slow painter. Even before the children came, she was a slow painter—painting and scraping the canvas clean and painting again. You just painted over something if you didn't like it until the thick paint became part of your aesthetic. For you, time has mostly been straightforward, a way of dividing the day neatly into segments. Only when you experimented with psychoactive drugs in your late teens—a long time ago now—did time become elastic. For her, though, time has often had an elastic quality, although the quality of this quality has changed. Time has now undergone a distinctive warping around parenthood, the way light is said to wrap around planets: the millennium of an afternoon spent pretending to be a Mommy when she is already, really, a Mommy; the bulb-bright flash of a kiss passed from one sibling to another, so quick she's not sure she saw it. The years fizzle, dissipate and blur. How can such short years have contained so many endless afternoons?

She does try to paint, though, when the children nap. Since they don't sleep at exactly the same time, her paintings get smaller and simpler, done in the minutes their naps overlap, and soon she's painting just with ink because it takes less prep time, and then she's not even using color because she can think more swiftly in black and white. She rediscovers an interest in Japanese landscape paintings because she can keep the simple brushstrokes in her head. She can paint and repaint these landscapes while she cooks, pushes a baby on the swing, drives the oldest to preschool: morning star and evening star, crescent moon, the shaded turning earth. You buy her books of haiku for her birthday, for inspiration. But practicing brushstrokes and reading haiku, she sees they're complex in ways that her brain doesn't seem capable of fathoming. "It always feels cluttered in here now," she says, pointing to her head. Her friends tell her that it's the hormones, that when she stops nursing, her head will clear.

When the kids get sick, throwing up, hallucinating from a high fever, you sit by their beds, empty their trashcans full of used tissues, hold their hair out of their faces as they vomit into a bowl. You spend all evening, until they finally fall asleep, until you can all fall asleep. In the middle of the night, you wake when you hear the barking cough of croup, but you find her already opening a window for the damp night air or bundling the coughing baby into the bathroom to breathe steam.

Finally, when the baby needs to be driven to the emergency room, you take him, and she stays with the others.

Once the youngest is a year old, she returns to teaching, but quickly gives it up again—at her part-time gigs, she earns less than you pay for childcare. She didn't want to give it up, those ten hours a week when she could apply her mind to someone else's children, and so for one semester, you tried trading off childcare. While she went to teach, you held office hours by phone, *Sesame Street* playing in the background. Neither of you had any painting time now though, and you both felt almost as exhausted as you had when the children were newborns. So you say to her, "Once they're in school, you'll have time. We'll order pizza every night. We'll let the laundry pile up all week. We won't bother washing the floors, ever." But even without teaching, even after the children are in school, she feels as if she doesn't have painting time.

In the afternoons, with their math sheets and spelling lists scattered over the kitchen table, the kids seem to spend hours bickering over toys or pencils, over nothing, over who gets to sit in which chair or choose the first cookie. She feels like Jimmy Carter, trying to get the Israelis and the Palestinians to negotiate. The day is successful if the negotiations have been polite; she's not even hoping for a workable outcome. While they argue, she puts her head in her hands, counts to ten, breathes so that she can feel her ribs move in and out, and then she raises her head and starts coaching the three of them toward reconciliation. "This will all be worth it," she tells herself. "Sometime."

After the children are in bed, she comes into the living room and you say, "What took so long?"

"Another story," she says, "with my hands doing shadow puppets on the wall. They all want me to make their birthday party invitations again this year, and books again for their birthdays too." She sighs. "They're not even very good books."

You don't understand. Why would she want to stop making those books—about soccer-playing bears, dancing cats, and minigolf courses where each hole is more fantastic than the next—underground bakeries, water hazards full of crocodiles, giant gumball machines intricate as atomic clocks? You love the drawings she does for these books, their quickness and simplicity and magic. You wish the children liked your stories and pictures as much as they like hers, but every time you start, they jump in to tell you that you don't know how to hold your hands just so in order to make the goose fly across the sky or that you don't really know how to draw a unicorn. You imagine that they don't do this to her.

"All my energy is going into illustrating those stories," she says. "Sometimes I think if I have to draw another traffic light or kitty cat, I'll scream." But sometimes when she doesn't reappear after putting the children to bed, you find her asleep with one of them, their hair tangled together on the pillow. Her breathing is as regular and even as a cat's and she's smiling. You let her sleep.

Even after she stops performing bedtime puppet shows, though, when the kids graduate from handmade books to Lego sets and computer games, she feels as if she doesn't have painting time—or no, time isn't really the issue. What is the issue, then? She's well aware that she's feeling sorry for herself—for no reason, she thinks, or she can't think of the reason, not right now, because it's time to go pick the middle one up from ballet, the youngest from soccer. She establishes a seven-thirty bedtime for all of them, even the oldest who's nine now, but when she goes into her studio in the evening, she finds herself sitting and staring at a blank wall, more unhappy every minute. Like the White Rabbit pulling out his pocket watch, she thinks, "I'll be late. I'll be late."

You take the children into your studio with you on Saturdays and let them draw with your charcoal or build sculptures out of stretcher scraps, telling them to be careful as you hand over the hammer and nails. The first few Saturdays, they work quietly on their own projects, and you wonder why she doesn't do this every day, just paint while they draw. Listening to them hum in the background, you feel happy, joyfully happy. Then one day, they stop getting along so well. The youngest threatens the oldest with the hammer and the oldest just laughs, and you have to step in. By the time the conflict is resolved—apparently a question of artistic idea stealing—all you can do is suggest a trip to the ice cream parlor.

One evening, she comes to your studio door. "There's nothing for dinner," she says.

"There are hotdogs in the freezer," you say.

"We can't eat another hotdog," she says, "I can't anyway," and she takes the kids and leaves for the grocery store even though maybe she could have spent that hour drawing instead.

She will look back on this as an era of crystal ball gazing, future divining, present regretting. That day in the grocery store, she caught an older woman staring at her children as they raced around, shopping lists in hand, tearing things off the shelves and dropping them into the cart—there and then gone. At the woman's sly smile, she said, "I know. They grow up so quickly and I need to enjoy them while I can. It's such a short time."

"Yes, dear," the older woman said wistfully. "They'll move out and you'll be so happy."

When you get promoted, you can finally afford a regular babysitter, after-school clubs, and summer camps. Even the youngest can go to day camp now, and she spends those mornings and early afternoons, between drop-off and pick-up, sitting in her half of the garage-studio, the half that's immaculately clean, staring out the window. Even the simplest brushstrokes have fled her brain. She draws one line, stops, and crunches the paper up. She draws with her eyes closed. She draws for fifteen minutes without lifting the pencil from the page. She takes something old and reworks it. She tries anything to get started but everything she generates looks like mud. When you ask if she wants to spend a warm afternoon at the lake, she says, "I don't know when this is going to happen." Her hands, by then, lie slack in her lap. "You have three hours," you tell her. "Pick up a brush. The painting will come."

One winter, her mother falls ill and she goes to care for her. As soon as it's certain her mother will recover, she realizes that she misses the touch of her children, the cold feet they tuck between her legs when they get into bed with her in the morning. And their smells: boy sweat, baby shampoo, garlic, sugar. Perhaps they've grown so much in the three weeks she's been gone she'll never get to experience those things again—a thought that fills her with anxiety.

When the kids are in high school, she has whole days to herself after their departure on the bus. She moves her studio down the street to an abandoned factory and leaves half-prepared dinners for your daughter to finish making. She tries not to think about how her teenagers are spending their time—probably just watching TV and doing their homework, she tells herself. She's finally painting—big black and brown paintings that come to her so quickly and powerfully she feels knocked over. The paintings look like burnt meat at first, but they evolve. They and she slow down until each individual brushstroke looks like a knit stitch or a purl, like the stitches she had looped endlessly together to make socks or sweaters while the children read their homework to her after dinner. Secretly she thinks of these paintings as a secret link to her family, a way of being with the children and away from them at the same time, and she's full of hope that someone else might feel their softness and prickliness. She works hard on these paintings—sometimes she doesn't even make it home in time for dinner—but she always feels she's playing catch-up. Your career has "taken off" as they say—museum shows, reviews in *Artforum*, the Whitney Biennial and then Basel and Venice, sales to big collectors who take you both out to dinner at restaurants that just make you feel uncomfortable. Every time she's asked, "Oh, do you paint too?" she smiles at them, smiles at you as you list all her accomplishments. She smiles until her cheeks ache. Sometimes, when she's not actually in her studio, she feels angry at the world, at you, at her children, which is a bad thing, not helpful, she tells herself, but she can't get rid of the resentment, ticking in her chest. If she can feel angry in her studio, that's better. There she can hold the brush in her hand and wait, like a time bomb, to go off, telling herself, "The only thing is to make this the best fucking painting in the world."

Later, years later, when she finally has a one-person show, a much younger painter asks her, "Would you have traded your children for a show at the Seattle Art Museum?" and she surprises herself by saying, suddenly and vehemently, "No!"

"At the Museum of Modern Art?"

"No!" she says again, even more vehemently.

Hunters and Gatherers

In the wading pool, that great cat eye, that circle half reflecting the blue summer sky and half-lidded with tree shadow, parents stand in water up to their knees and make sure their toddlers don't drown. It's a bright hot Sunday. Elsewhere in the park, blue-haired ladies in red suits visit the orchids in the conservatory, middle-aged lovers watch a production of *A Midsummer Night's Dream* set in a Vegas casino, scholars enter the Asian Art Museum, couples lie together on the grass, tanning their identical backs, teenagers smoke weed behind the bandstand and text their friends. Around the wading pool, mothers nurse infants in the shade. Older children splash each other, long arcs of water.

An arc lands on Anna and her already damp beach towel. She sits on one Ninja Turtle, while her older son sprawls on the other, playing with two army guys as he calls them, which he's snuck out of the house. In this neighborhood where almost every car—including hers—sports an antiwar bumper sticker, his mother suspects he single-handedly buys out the stock of army guys at the local 99-cent store, bag after giant bag of olive-green men, their heads and hands the same color as their clothes. At home, he sets up battles across the living room and kitchen, his soldiers marching in neat rows from the couch to the TV and from the back door, across the linoleum and hardwood, and then up the ladder-back chairs until the opposing platoons meet on the dining room table. He begs to be allowed to leave them there until one side or the other proves their strategy stronger—no mind for the impending meal. "Please, please can't we eat at the counter just this once?" He's not supposed to take them out of the house, but today he has snuck several into the capacious pockets of his bathing suit, and he now lies on his stomach setting up a miniversion of one of the battles he designs at home. He'd like to pretend that his mother's toenails, painted a vivid deep pink, are land mines for the guys to dodge around but he knows better. Then he flips over onto his back and two of the guys engage in combat on his white stomach. His mother has opened the Week in Review section of the *New York Times*, and she can hear the sound effects of hand-to-hand combat, fitting, she thinks, as background music for the article she's reading about the state of the war in Iraq. Then her son says, "You know what should happen to Barbie? G.I. Joe should gun her down. He should get in the Barbie car and run her over. He should burn down the Barbie house." Privately, his mother thinks that this might be a good thing to happen to Barbie, to all Barbies worldwide with their permanently tippy-toe feet and gravity-defying breasts, but she says, "That's horrible. Where do you come up with these things?" She can feel her son shrug and then she hears the sound of plastic attacking plastic again. What should happen to G.I. Joe in return? Squashed by a giant Hello Kitty doll, she thinks and leans in close over her newspaper so that her son won't see her laugh. She'll tell her husband about this later—he's at a baseball game with his buddies—and they'll laugh together. And, really, she's pleased she hasn't had girls: all that pink, all that Barbie, the princess thing. Apparently, there's an endless princess thing, although she doesn't remember going through one herself.

"The most popular reconstruction of early human social behavior is summarized in the phrase 'man the hunter.' In this hypothesis meat eating initiated man's separation from the apes. Males provided the meat, presumed to be the main item in early hominid diet, by inventing stone tools and weapons for hunting. Thus males played the major economic role, were protectors of females and young, and controlled the mating process. In this view of things, females fade into a strictly reproductive and passive role."[1]

Across the pool, Anna's friend Martha wears a golden princess crown. It glitters on her head where her four-year-old daughter has placed it pre-

---

1. Adrienne L. Zihlman, "Women as Shapers of the Human Adaptation," in *Woman the Gatherer*, ed. Frances Dahlberg (New Haven, CT: Yale University Press, 1981), 75.

cariously. The girl is now clinging to her leg like a limpet, relentless in pursuit of her mother's love. "Please," she's whining, "please play princess with me. You're the queen and I'm the princess and Daddy is the Daddy but he's back at the castle." Her best friend, a boy she usually calls "the prince," comes over and levels pistol-shaped fingers at her head. "Bang," he says, and she swats him away. Later, cold from splashing in the water all afternoon, he holds out his arms to her. "Huggy?" he says. She turns away and crosses her arms over her chest. "No," she says.

Apparently, meat makes up a large part of male chimpanzees' diets, and male chimps have the agility and strength to chase down and kill arboreal monkeys. Female chimps, on the other hand, "specialize in gathering social insects," "[fishing] for termites over three times as frequently as males." They do this quietly, in a single location.[2]

In the sun, two women sit with arms around each other in a loose hug. They eat chips with salsa dipped from a plastic tub, and watch their boy share his floaty frog with littler kids in the pool. They're feeling good, pleased by his generosity. Later, he comes over, sits in one Mom's lap, his suit immediately soaking her, and grabs a handful of chips. "What are you talking about?" he asks.

"This and that," she says. "What do you want to talk about?"

"Guns and weapons," he says. "You know all those pirate swords I have? He just told me"—he points to another little boy—"that pirates fought with cutlasses, not swords, and they used blunderbusses, not pistols."

The women look at each other. They sense their home arsenal will be expanding.

Reconnaissance: girls in a line collect treasures. Martha's daughter is off to join them in their search for miniature toy animals, plastic babies, rings from the gum machine, beads they dig out of the playground sand

2. W. C. McGrew, "The Female Chimpanzee as a Human Evolutionary Prototype," in Dahlberg, *Woman the Gatherer*, 44, 50.

with a stick, special tiny pinecones, pretty rocks, single sequins, broken shells, flower petals, bottle caps, all put into purses—they can never have enough purses. Martha's daughter's favorite book involves a purple plastic purse which contains two quarters, never spent, along with glittery movie star sunglasses. Useless things. "Let me get out my jewelry box," she says to her mother most mornings. "Which one?" Martha wonders, restraining herself from petting her daughter's lovely black hair.

Now, watching the line of girls in their frilly bathing suits, a thought comes to her, suddenly and with great understanding: They're gathering. Oh my god, they're gathering.

The girls' line stops moving, and Martha's daughter turns back, forward again, back. Giggling, she reaches one dirty hand forward, another back and draws the two hands she finds together with her own. Three popsicle-sticky sets of fingers doing what? Martha wonders. Clasping? Some sort of affectionate pinching?

After the mission has succeeded, Martha's daughter brings one of the other little girls over. "Momma, can we have a playdate?" she says. Just the other day in the car, she'd been bemoaning the fact that she'd be going off to a new school in the fall. She'd miss her friends. "You'll make new ones, honey," Martha reassured and listened to the intense silence in the back seat for a while, until finally her daughter said, "Yes, and then I can connect my old friends to my new ones."

"In general, newborn boys are more physically active and more vigorous, while newborn girls are quieter, and more responsive to faces and voices. Typically, boys are more aggressive, girls more social; boys respond more to objects, girls to people."[3]

Martha's older girl, her eleven-year-old, now wears a bikini and carries a cell phone. She's lying in the sun, texting her best friend, and listening to her iPod. Martha can hear Avril Lavigne's tinny voice leaking out of the earbuds and taps her daughter's arm. "Turn it down," she mouths.

---

3. Arlene Eisenberg, Heidi Murkoff, and Sandee Hathaway, *What to Expect: The Toddler Years* (New York: Workman Publishing Co., 1994), 223.

When she sees the videos—super short skirts, pink-streaked hair, rings of black eye makeup—she thinks, My god, she should still be listening to Peter, Paul & Mary.

Apparently, according a study published recently in *Current Biology*, women *do* prefer pink, a throwback to the days when they were responsible for gathering the ripest fruit and berries, while the men were out bringing down Mastodons.[4]

Anna looks up, assuring herself that her younger boy is still safely on the playground, sending his wooden train down the slide. There he is, with the current favorite engine, white Fearless Freddie with its red cow catcher, black wheels, and two golden smokestacks. He holds it high above his head as another boy jumps for it, shouting, "It's my turn now. You promised. You promised." The boy's face is turning an angry red. Anna sighs. If her son doesn't give in soon, she'll go over before one of the kids gets whacked with the train or sits down at the top of the slide in tears. She'll facilitate a negotiation, although she never thought her legal training would lead to this, just this, only this. Still, it makes more sense for her to stay home with the kids for a while, while her husband stays a lawyer. And she'll take another engine in her pocket so that they can each have one in case the negotiation doesn't pan out.

"When individuals collect foods which they transport and exchange with others, social relationships become paramount. . . . Males can afford to invest time and energy [in hunting] beyond a certain point only if they can count on collected food from females being available when they return empty handed. In this sense, females were the facultative sex, and in the tropics male big-game hunting relied on female gathering, rather than vice versa. An important advance occurred when mothers continued to share food with offspring after weaning. This led to sharing among matrilines and eventually enabled food to be distributed in the reverse direction, from offspring to parent. Such reciprocity

---

4. Anya C. Hurlbert and Yazhu Ling, "Biological Components of Sex Differences in Color Preference," *Current Biology* 17, no. 16 (August 2007), R623–R625.

allowed younger individuals to profit from the accumulated knowledge of elders who otherwise would not have survived."[5]

Martha watches kids play catch in the field. It seems that girls throw from the wrist, the ball destined to form a high unstable arc and float to the ground, a soft lob that can land an apple perfectly in a basket, while boys throw from the elbow, making for more effective follow-through, good for driving a spear right into a deer's heart. She thinks how when a softball pitcher sends her fastball toward the plate, the commentators comment on the angle of her hips. Baseball commentators never mention Roger Clemens's hips or Felix Hernandez's hips. For them it's all arm and shoulder. But, man, some of those college softball pitchers are amazing—endless strikeouts thrown and endless home runs hit in the same game.

Anna's older son has brought Pokémon cards to the park too, and he now sits at the edge of the wading pool with his feet in the water, showing them to a girl from his school. Before he hands a card over for inspection, he waves it in the air or rubs it on his damp chest or on a dry spot on the concrete. "That will keep them from getting ruined," he says. "We don't want to get them wet. Mom says she won't buy any more just because I get them wet." The girl has her own deck with her, and they look at each others' cards for a while, until the girl says, "Do you want this one? I don't want it anymore."

He sees that it's a Rhyperion Level X, a mean-looking brown creature with two horns on its head, and snatches it eagerly out of her hand. "This?" he says. "Are you sure? It's got 170 HP. I can beat anybody with this one, even a Torterra."

"It's OK," she says.

"I can just have it?" he asks. He can't believe his luck, imagining this new card snuck into his theme deck, poised for the next Poké battle.

"You can have it," she says. "I only want the cute ones. This one isn't cute enough."

---

5. McGrew, "The Female Chimpanzee," 60–61.

Apparently, men buy and women shop, according to researchers at the Wharton School's Jay H. Baker Retail Initiative and the Verde Group, a Toronto consulting firm: that is, men enter a store with a specific target in mind and carry out their mission as quickly as possible, while women enter a store for the experience of touching the merchandise, meandering, comparing, chatting with the saleswomen.[6] But Anna has done her own share of guerilla shopping over the years: stride into the store, snatch what you need, tap your foot impatiently as the cashier makes small talk, exit. And her husband loves to linger, discussing the freshest seafood or the best band saw, or choosing the juiciest steak.

While Anna and Martha feed the kids snacks—slices of apple and Pirate's Booty, a sort of PC version of Cheetos they've decided, a horde of teenagers comes whooping down the hill, boys and girls identical with their blue and pink hair, their studded wristbands and studded belts and pierced septa. Good-naturedly they roll up their pant legs and leap into the pool where they begin a game in which a "tag" consists of a full body slam, sending the victim flat out into the water. This is followed by the tagger extending a hand to help the other person up, and lots of laughing. Little kids sit in the water wide-eyed, and parents scoop up babies, harrumphing at the invasion. Once all the teenagers have gotten soaked, they head across the street to play kickball with some elementary school kids. The boys take off their ripped black T-shirts to use for the bases. They all hop up and down with glee when they get a run.

"They're not so bad," Martha thinks, handing over another juice box, despite all she's heard about friends with benefits, drug use, and blow jobs involving dark red lipstick. She wishes she'd had an adolescence like that, full of raucous fun, rather than one which alternated between bookish seclusion and tawdry love affairs.

Summers, when Anna and Martha were barely teenagers, they played poker with the boys from the camp across the lake. Every time the boys

---

6. "[TS]'Men Buy, Women Shop': The Sexes Have Different Priorities When Walking Down the Aisles," *Knowledge@Wharton*, November 28, 2007, http://knowledge.wharton.upenn.edu/article.cfm?articleid=1848.

asked if they could play strip poker, and every time the girls said no. After the boys had left, they retreated to Anna's bunk and talked about how their children would wear striped overalls and hand-knit socks, eat only homemade bread, play with wooden cars and rag dolls. They listened to "Teach Your Children" and "Our House" and dreamed they would live in that house, with the cats and the yard and the fireplace and the beloved children. Were they dreaming of being the parents in that house or of still being the children? This was before they'd had sex with anyone, when their closest contact with a boy—other than the poker players—was Martha's younger brother Bill, who, despite the fact that he sometimes liked to rip towels off their naked bodies, seemed quite harmless. This was before they'd come into contact with anyone— male or female—who could be considered harmful in any way.

"Having children means constantly stepping on tiny pieces of plastic," Martha says as she invites Anna in later that afternoon and they avoid the scattered Barbie shoes embedded in the living room carpet.

"You could just not buy the Barbie stuff," Anna says, and Martha gives her a wry look, patting her friend's purse, stuffed with toy cars and trains and the army guys that have fallen out of her son's bathing suit pockets.

Privately, Martha admits that she's glad she didn't have a boy. "That gun thing. I don't know how I'd deal with it," she says.

"Remember Bill?" Anna says. "Remember how he was really into guns?"

"Oh yeah. From like the time he was three until he graduated from high school. I guess he turned out okay."

The kids plop themselves down around the kitchen table to wait for lemonade, knocking over the piles of clean clothes Martha's husband has spent the morning folding. He'd spent all of Saturday loading and unloading the washer and dryer, the week's worth of eight loads of laundry. And the day before that, he'd left work early to take both girls to the dentist while Martha sat in an endless Friday afternoon meeting.

"Did you know," her younger girl says now, "that if you find a four-leaf clover, you should pick it because it's magic? Did you know that you can catch an elf with one? If there's dew on one, he'll want to drink it. You just need to sit really really still and hold out your hand like this, and then he'll come up and you can look right in his face, just like at a little doll." Then she laughs uproariously, and the other kids stare at her as if she's crazy.

She already has a dollhouse that she never plays with, as do Anna's boys. Anna has bought them baby dolls to nurture, and although they sometimes like to dress up in her discarded party dresses—a lacy black number with a sweetheart neckline or a maroon chiffon with cap sleeves—they've shown no interest in the dolls. Martha's older daughter had played with the dollhouse, fashioning furniture out of match-boxes, marshmallows, and spools of thread. Her younger one has fairy dolls collecting dust on a shelf and Polly Pocket dolls with innumerable flexible plastic outfits that never get changed, My Little Ponies whose long pastel-colored manes and tails she refuses to brush with the tiny matching hairbrushes. She also has a double dump truck she fails to drive around their backyard sandbox, and an electric train her father plays with at Christmas, setting it up under their tree. She much prefers an imaginative game in which she's the director of her own potion-making school. During these games, she empties their basement of dead bugs and fills their kitchen with the competing odors of bakeshop and chemical laboratory. She has designed badges for all her students to wear and recipes for the potions they must learn to make in levels of dif-ficulty ranging from red up through the colors of the rainbow to purple. She has requested that her most recent birthday cake be in the shape of a cauldron, never mind how the black frosting will stain her guests' teeth.

"Extensive sharing of food other than meat requires containers to accu-mulate and transport the food. Humans today, particularly women, carry both food and infants and must have carried them in the past; and many scholars have suggested that women must have invented carrying devices. But their containers are perishable, being made generally of flexibles such as bark, grass, folded leaves, animal skins, which leave no trace in the archeological record. . . . McGrew and Zihlman remind us that the late appearance of stone tools and their association with hunting does not mean that hominids were not using perishable tools and containers and sharing food much earlier."[7]

Anna scaled cliffs as a teenager, leaving both Bill and Martha behind, then dove from the cliff tops, belly flopping into the cold ocean below.

Martha's younger daughter loves any sparkly object; her older daughter is the shyest person she knows and has only one friend, now moved away (hence, the cell phone). She prefers to spend her time alone, hitting a tennis ball against the garage wall or swimming laps in Lake Washington.

And Anna's boys gather things too: wooden trains, plastic construction vehicles, toy dinosaurs, Pokémon cards, baseball cards, Lego minifigures. They gather all sorts of arcane knowledge to go along with the objects, not just the dinosaurs but their names and when they lived and what they ate and how big they were. They know how a steam engine works, how a lightsaber works, the difference between a digger and a loader, the ERA of every Mariner's pitcher, what HP means and all the convoluted rules for the game they play with those cards.

"In the northernmost section of Isabela and well into Cagayan province, women are active and proficient hunters. . . . On the Dianggu [River], some of the women questioned, and observed hunting, carried machetes and were accompanied by dogs. They claim to prefer the machete to the bow and arrow, allowing dogs to corner and hold pigs for sticking with the knife.

On the Malibu River, Agta women are expert bow and arrow hunters. On both of our brief visits to this group, women were observed hunting. They claim to use bows always, and they seek the full range of prey animals. Informants say they hunt only with dogs. On closer questioning they admit to knowing techniques that do not involve dogs— for example, they may climb trees and lie in wait for an animal to approach to feed on fallen fruit.[8]

---

7. Frances Dahlberg, introduction to Dahlberg, *Woman the Gatherer*, 8–9.

8. Agnes Estioko-Griffin and P. Bion Griffin, "Woman the Hunter: The Agta," in Dahlberg, *Woman the Gatherer*, 128–29.

Over in the pool, a man tips his daughter upside down so that her hair swings in the water and her laughter rings, until all the kids around her run to their fathers and ask for a dunking too. Or for a nose to be wiped or a swollen finger to be kissed. Or for chips to eat or a story to hear. And the fathers oblige.

Never mind yellow bananas . . . Orange oranges . . . Fuzzy green kiwi . . . Blue-violet blueberries . . . And everyone—male and female—apparently prefers blue, because blue sky means good weather.[9] Everyone apparently, except for Anna's younger son who dresses only in red, from shirt to socks, always chooses the sparkly ruby slippers in Nordstrom and is always disappointed when his mother says no. Not that she really cares, but she cares that others might tease him and then he'd care and then he'd lose his charming and beautiful interest in red and sparkles.

Gathering, hunting, trading, sale: if human society and its elaborate social interactions began with the sharing of food, then Anna's oldest fully participates in a slightly later stage, a barter economy. He'll offer a blue stegosaurus for a red T. rex, a Darth Vader Lego figure for a Harry Potter. He tried to trade that girl something for her Rhyperion card—a Swablu maybe, that little yellow bird with cloudlike wings, or a Shaymin with Flower Aroma and Hibiscus ears—but she'd said no. He participates in the cash economy too, saving his allowance to buy a special toy, but the process of taking money to the store does not enrapture him nearly as much as making the perfect trade with one of his friends. Are trade and barter forms of social interchange?

Is the pursuit of the shiniest jewel a form of hunting?

Martha's youngest takes part in a gift economy, in which all objects are reflective only of love. She makes trinkets out of pipe cleaners and wraps them up in tissues, elaborately taped together, then gives them to her parents. She gives her favorite toy teacups to her babysitter, jewels to her friends, grief to her big sister who still can't get over the ignominy of her birth, but then also her favorite necklace—a string of pink glass beads and a larger pink glass heart, a fairy heart she says.

---

9. Hurlbert and Ling, "Biological Components," R623–R625.

"Math class is tough!" Barbie said in 1992, when she also said, "Will we ever have enough clothes?" and "I love shopping." But apparently math isn't tough anymore for girls, or no tougher than it is for boys. According to a study funded by the National Science Foundation, math scores show no gap for girls.[10] Girls perform as well as boys on standardized tests. And apparently math isn't tough for Anna's older daughter who discovered the Fibonacci Sequence on her own in kindergarten: "$0 + 1 = 1, 1 + 1 = 2, 1 + 2 = 3$," she sang. "$2 + 3 = 5, 3 + 5 = 8$." And her mother and father sat listening, imagining the spirals of pinecones and shells, the flowerings of artichokes, the curve of waves. Now there is even a *Barbie Starting Math* workbook for kids entering kindergarten. "Youngsters will love learning math skills from Barbie, who is the ideal role model wherever she goes," reads the promo material.[11] And indeed, Barbie has now had more than eighty careers, ranging from teenage fashion model to veterinarian to Olympic athlete to presidential candidate to medic sergeant enlisted in Desert Storm. Barbie has been an astronaut three times, most recently in 1994 when she carried a sparkly silver purse into outer space. There can never be enough purses.

Martha swore she'd never dress a girl in pink but her daughters both loved pink and looked delicious in it, like strawberry ice cream cones. When she was getting her master's degree in civil engineering, she herself had loved to wear a bright pink sweater given to her by her uncle. One rainy day as she walked across campus, her favorite professor, the first woman to design a major bridge, caught up with her. "Ah, pink," her professor said, tapping her pink shoulder and passing her by. "I haven't worn pink since the revolution started." And Martha stopped, staring after her teacher's tan trench coat, her gray hair tucked under a clear plastic hood, and wondered what revolution she was talking about. Then, "Ah," she thought, with the click of recognition. "The

---

10. Tamar Lewin, "Math Scores Show No Gap for Girls, Study Finds," *New York Times*, July 25, 2008.

11. Copy text for *Barbie Kindergarten Workbook: Starting Math*, QBD Books website, https://www.qbd.com.au/barbie-kindergarten-workbook-starting-math/various/9780330378130/.

feminist revolution. I take so much for granted." She'd kept wearing the pink sweater, though, until it fell apart. And when she'd found out she was pregnant with a girl, she'd decided that her girl children could choose pink for themselves, once they were grown-ups, but she wouldn't buy it for them. And that vow had lasted just about as long as the others she'd made before the children were real: that she'd never let them cry themselves to sleep, that she'd never lose her temper or feel like giving one of them a swift slap on the rear, that she'd never say "Because I'm the mother, that's why," that she'd never bribe them with sugar, TV, or a new toy.

"*Both* sexes must have been able to care for young, protect themselves from predators, make and use tools, and freely move about the environment in order to exploit available resources widely distributed through space and time. It is this range of behaviors—the overall behavioral flexibility of both sexes—that may have been the *primary* ingredient of the early hominids' success. . . ."[12]

And Anna's younger son, the unexpected—OK, the accident—the one who kisses his trucks good night before he gets into bed. One minute he's making the vroom-vroom noise of the engines and the next he's arranging the trucks into families: Mommy, Daddy, brother, baby brother, baby baby brother (he wants one of these), dog, cat, canary. Although they've never had a pet of any kind (discounting her older son's Mexican jumping bean), he's sure a canary must be part of any family, in this case represented by a diminutive yellow checker cab her sister sent him from New York City. What does she make of him? And the older one with army guys stuffed into his pockets—he's named the jumping bean Fred and built him a house, complete with comfy cotton ball furniture and a painted palm tree outside to make him feel at home. Before leaving for day camp in the morning, he quite seriously tells her: "Make sure to put Fred in the fridge at noon for his nap." What does she make of him?

---

12. Zihlman, "Women as Shapers," 97.

The Arches, Our Home

Once, long ago, my darlings, Shilshole was one door and Alki another, and when they swung open, seawater came rushing in from the Puget Sound. Through those doors also came fish and mollusks, crawling or scrabbling or swimming up through the salty waves and some of them even onto land, sucking up muddy pebbles and old pinecones. Back then, fish could sing. The giant horse conch's whorls, cords, and ribs remained orange throughout its long life; and the giant triton, now a mere twenty inches in length, was truly a giant. Pisaster giganteus's five legs were studded with blue jewels. The sunflower sea star had even more arms than the twenty-four it has today, and when each signed separately, you could watch it talking to itself, waving those powerful suckers around. Back then, coral creatures could swim—or walk—or perform one of those moves where you take gigantic off-kilter steps along a silty bottom and make swimming motions with your arms: not quite fish, not quite fowl, not quite frog. The fishier fish jumped in the shallows and the landier mollusks scrambled or sunbathed on the beach. Then the doors would swing the other way, and back to sea all the creatures would rush. "Last one out's a rotten egg," the youngest would say, thinking perhaps of his unripe siblings, drying out on the rocks.

In the Marianas Trench, a giant belched heat and carbonic acid into the water. In the landlocked central plains of every continent, giants raked away mountains and others spewed ash into the air. On a far-off island, a giant pushed the water with fallen palms lashed together into a paddle. Shells weakened. Coral bleached. Seagrass died. Waves barreled and broke and the sea level rose and rose.

The doors opened, but the timing was not as the creatures remembered. Perhaps a malfunction in the tidal mechanism or the latest creakifying whoosh of hot acidic water had damaged the hinges. Some days waves rushed in with unprecedented force and muscled themselves out with extraordinary power, while other days water trickled in too slowly and oozed out again like treacle. Sometimes the mussels, clams, conchs, whelks, tritons, and starfish found themselves stranded along the seawall or just below the sculpture park, and had to wait for the next high tide to dislodge them. Each time they waited longer—for the next full moon or the next new moon or a storm surge or just for that mythical larger seventh wave. Sometimes the fish said, "Come on, guys. Time to get going," but you know, my darlings, my little ones, that even you don't always listen to your well-meaning friends and so you can imagine how those large slow creatures with their tiny brains reacted to this advice.

Higher and higher ashore the big waves washed them. Longer and longer it took them to return home to the water. More and more often they found themselves stranded far from the sea. Over time they ossified, making room first for all sorts of tiny mammals, and finally humans who moved into the empty shells like hermit crabs. In the winter, when the cold rain came down in torrents, children slid down the interior whorls of the conchs. In spring, parents propped open the doors of their mussel homes to let in the air, and in the summer, everyone bathed in the clean shallow pools that collected in upturned limpets. In those days before milk, people got their calcium by chipping away at their homes and placing the chips under their tongues.

Over time, though, the houses crumbled. Condos replaced shells everywhere, and as we moved from the natural forms into the four-square ones, our lives became less fluid too, less joyous, I dare say. I hear you now, my darlings. You say, "I'll never live in a box house," but then, where will you live? The shells are all gone, and their metallic replacements shine too hotly in the sun and the air inside of them tastes like dirty pennies. Only the Science Center arches remain, the last real thing, vestiges of the leafy sea dragon, now a fish no larger than a teacup but back then . . . They came and dried, a skeleton of lace, a napkin of knits, a Florentine cookie, a wedding veil of skin and now stone.

Six Views of Seattle

I

In the middle of the hospital sits the operating room, between the birthing suites and the postpartum rooms; between the empty football stadium, the mansions in Laurelhurst, bits of water scattered with canoes and herons, beavers and turtles; and the Montlake Cut, where boats clamor so that the bridge will swing up and they can continue their summer cruise from Lake Washington to Lake Union. There, in the middle room, the needle pricked the spine and the scalpel sliced. There, in the cold middle room: blue walls, blue scrubs, blue masks, blue steel, blue baby. The doctors and nurses, breathing easily, pulled the baby out, blue until he screamed, and his father took him away to be washed and wrapped and to become pink, the desired color for newborns. And then I—because he'd been sliced out of *me*—I was permitted to see him, his most beautiful face and his most beautiful slate-blue eyes and his most beautiful pink mouth attempting a phantom smile. Before his birth, there had been some conflict over the necessity for a C-section, a conflict the baby's father and I had not participated in but which had churned quietly between the nurse who said, "With time, her body will figure out how to birth this baby," and the doctor who said, "I don't think he's going anywhere; she could push for three more hours and *then* we could do the C-section," until my husband and I had nodded "yes" to each other, and I looked at them and said, "Now please. I want to see the baby now."

II

Tear it down and build condos—or no, build a park, a vast greensward—or an amphitheater or a museum or a radio station or covered parking—or no, keep it, keep it. The Fun Forest (with its ancient Windstorm roller-coaster, its rickety merry-go-round, games of darts, indoor minigolf course including a mini–Space Needle, and its Ferris wheel that provides views of the real Space Needle just next door, and of all the rest of Seattle, from Queen Anne Hill, across Elliott Bay to Alki, down toward the docks, and even, when the clouds lift, over Puget Sound to the Olympics, already capped with snow)—what, in the middle of the city, is it a forest of? Through the drizzle, watch little figures, families, parents and children in matching slickers, and follow one, then another, to read their thoughts. They climb into the Ferris wheel's gondolas, ride on carousel horses, clamber into the spinning airplanes, slide down the splashing log ride, toss darts at the balloons, and shoot water into the toy clowns' open mouths. This girl wants a hot dog for lunch and that boy bemoans the fact that his mother won't give him another five dollars to spend on Skee-Ball, and that father there dreads his soggy bike ride to work on Monday, but when they get home they will all sit down together at the kitchen table and write letters pleading for the Fun Forest, licking the freshly sharpened tips of their pencils and writing, because the kids love the sound those balloons make when they pop and love the cheap stuffed animals and giant inflatable Tweety birds they win and love the thrill of the rattling steel coaster, and because the parents remember that they had their first kiss—not with the person they're currently married to—on that Ferris wheel; and down at city hall the following week, the city council members will receive the letters, and even though they have a soft spot in their hearts for the Fun Forest, they know that it hasn't paid its bills for years and that only 3 percent of visitors say they enjoy the place, and so after they reply to each of the letters with an autographed photo and the promise to consider its requests deeply, they burn the letters rather than filing them away. That night there are nine fires in nine office wastepaper baskets, like the lights of nine campfires in the autumn woods, and the city council members dream red dreams—the red of a clown's tongue, of a painted horse's mane, of paper amusement park tickets, of maple leaves turned, and of fire, the sparkle of sparks that drift up toward the patternless blinking of red lights atop the Space Needle, the bloodshot eye of a single beneficent god—and they know that the decision they have made is a good one, that the parents will remember those kisses anyway and the children will skate on the new skating rink in their red winter coats happily, and someday the new skating rink will grow old, and the new climbing sculpture will grow red with rust, and the trees of nostalgia will grow again.

III

At the corner of Aurora and Denny, bright pink neon lights and a giant twirling cartoon elephant beckon through the December rain and the early dark. In the car, a struggle, a skirmish, between getting Pokie, the toy elephant, RIGHT NOW, from the grocery store where he'd disappeared that morning and getting the car washed first. It's this "first" that the backseat passenger doesn't understand, and she kicks her mother's seat as hard as she can, then defeated, sits in her booster, sucking her thumb and staring out the window as they turn corner after corner, her other hand toying with the edge of the fluffy magenta skirt she's worn for visiting Grandma, whom she stays with every Saturday night, weekdays being busy with preschool, gymnastics, playdates, and Kindermusik. At the car wash, the Pink Elephant Car Wash, she stands on a chair in the atrium and watches through a window as the spraying water and squirting soap and automatic brushes wash the cars clean like a living holiday display, and when the machines are done, she hands the ticket and tip to the man who has so carefully removed all her trash from the backseat. Later, she'll take Pokie into the bath with her even though this will make him lumpy, rub his head and scrub behind his ears and down his tummy, wash between all four of his legs, and finally use the handheld shower to rinse all the soap from his pink fur. Now she turns and looks out the back window and squints until the pink lights blur like a million Christmas lights and the spinning elephants turn into one elephant—Goodbye car wash!—and she thinks about Pokie's soft trunk until she can feel it in her fist, and how she'll take that trunk and poke her brother with it, and she remembers how yummy it was to kick the back of her mother's seat since she's only just gotten tall enough to reach it with her sneaker-clad feet.

IV

We watch the little ones run over from the path, whooping like the crazy monkeys at sunset, their hot breath steaming in the cold air, and we wait for them, snarling and scratching the glass with our big paws. On their heads, they have long fur—brown or black or yellow—and from their backs they take off the fur in colors we don't know the names of and show us the meat, like that rabbit, the one that didn't get away, whose brown fur we ripped off and whose meat and bones we ate, but we have thick brown fur everywhere that no one, ever, will rip from us and that keeps us warm even in this cold that reminds us of Alaska, except that we have never been to Alaska despite our name. Controlled though we don't want to be, prodded awake in the winter, required to forage for scattered food, encouraged to follow the scent of hidden elk droppings or cinnamon until we've learned to recognize the smell of oatmeal cookies, we might just fight that stick held out to keep us away when the food arrives (wait to eat? but we're starving!); when the little ones run up the path, the big one pulls on a string tied around all their waists and they come back to her if they don't tumble first. "You little animals, when will you learn what separates us from them?" she says, jerking her chin toward us, and when one of them growls, "I want to learn how to be a bear," she says: "Speak English, please." In the snow, they've come to the zoo to see the wolves and the mountain goats, elk, river otters, snowy owls, arctic foxes, bald eagles, and us, of course us, mostly us, in a cage fashioned into something that doesn't look like a cage, because they can't go see us out there where we belong, where they belong. If the keepers knew that we knew the meaning of that stick and how fragile it was, and if the teachers knew that bears could understand the human tongue, they'd be shocked, but we bears have learned our lessons well: don't roar when the school groups come or the children will deafen us with their screams, catch fish for the families on Saturday, take cover on the other side of the hill when the staring is too much, and bide your time; someday this glass will crack.

V

Ten, with a belly the other kids haven't started teasing him about yet, the boy has skipped school today, put on his favorite green windbreaker with the fleece lining, and pushed his blond hair off his forehead. Perhaps, dear reader, if we follow him, we'll discover his plan, learn his reasons for hiding behind a bush when the school bus turns the corner and then rushing to the city bus stop instead. See him there, waiting in front of Safeway for the Number 43 and the trip downtown where, I'm quite sure, he'll head directly to Pike Place Market with its sellers of fish and squeaky cheese, tulips and daffodils, sausages, peapods and young garlic shoots, and its views of the ferries crossing the Sound on this glittering spring day. Green, he's hidden behind the lighter green of lettuce leaves and the darker green of broccoli rabe, the green globes of artichokes and grapes transported from California. Ah, he's buying food for his father's birthday dinner, since his mother stormed out of the house two days ago, and the thought of Dad with no favorite food for his birthday has led the boy down here, to watch the men toss fish to each other and to decide between salmon and clams, John Dory and shrimp, the season's first halibut and a nice mountain trout, for he's a sweet boy, wouldn't you agree? and he wants this dinner to be perfect although he really has no idea how to cook it and wishes wishes wishes his mother were there to teach him instead of off somewhere—who knows where? not even us—after their fight. After buying his ingredients, he'll ride the bus back home and have all day to wash, chop, braise, simmer, steam, and grill, and hope the fish cooks through without burning, before setting the table and frosting the chocolate cake he's baked from a mix, spreading the green buttercream and decorating it with spun sugar goals and plastic soccer players.

VI

Eight o'clock, nine o'clock, ten o'clock on a summer evening—it's time to close the eyes, allow the breath to deepen, and sleep. The neighbor's cat sleeps under the camellia bush and the neighbor's baby has given up her screaming and sleeps in her crib; the hummingbird babies sleep in their nest perched on the Christmas-light wire strung across the porch ceiling; boys and girls everywhere put on their pajamas and brush their teeth; grandparents, all four of them, rest underground. In this house, though, the children call for glasses of water, kick off their sheets and pull them back up, ask for stories about the grandparents they've never met, count airplanes going in for a landing at SeaTac, their red lights blinking down through the trees, tell each other jokes through their open bedroom doors, and throw pillows at any parent who dares suggest it's time for sleep. Yes, darlings, you're right: while light still fills the sky and the first star appears and then the others, and while your parents sit on the porch steps with their glasses of wine, trading stories, it's impossible to think that this vast middle—life—will ever end, that anything will ever die. Now, before dark sets in, watch all the colors fade to gray: the last stripe of orange sunset in the west; the blue sky pulsating overhead; the cedar and eucalyptus and dogwood all dissolving into dark—a gray and then a darker gray that is the color of our house walls, headstones, and stormwater rushing over Snoqualmie Falls. At the falls today, after playing in the hot sun and the icy rocky river bed, attempting to catch minnows, you hiked the slowest hike in all creation back up the steep slope you'd run down an hour before, scuffing the gray dust with your toes, and moaning about your aching legs and parched throats and sweaty backs and lack of ice cream, but once we got back to the city, you decided you hadn't had enough of the outdoors and insisted we stop in Volunteer Park where you, Ezra Jacob (grandson of Jack and great-grandson of Jake) and Phoebe Rose (granddaughter of Phoebe and great-granddaughter of Rose), sat side by side on the swings and pumped yourselves up and up and almost out over the fence separating the playground from the cemetery, out over blackberry bushes and hydrangeas, out over the chain link and then the short clipped grass and the monuments, so that if you'd let go, you would have sailed toward a waiting angel who would lift her stone arms and catch you, happy for the chance to save someone, happy for the reprieve from guarding a grave.

Annunciation

Her feet up in the stirrups, waiting for the doctor to return and for the cold prod of the speculum, Judith heard the scream come from the room next door. These days, her thoughts immediately went to cancer: breast cancer, uterine cancer, or the worst, ovarian cancer. Her closest friend had recently succumbed to that one. But when Dr. _____ (*How could she forget his name? She's been seeing him for years!*) gave that perfunctory knock and came into the room, glancing at the chart in his hand, he was chuckling to himself. "How are you today, Mrs. Cooperman?" he asked, still chuckling, and proceeded to don the plastic gloves and goop them up so that his hand could slide right up inside her. No one had placed a finger inside her for a while though she couldn't decide whether she missed it or just missed missing it. Bernard had been gone for nearly twenty years, off with that "floozy," as Judith couldn't help calling the other, newer Mrs. Cooperman, although she knew it was a word left over from movies she sat through during her teens in the 1940s. Since he left, she'd been quite virginal, she thought.

Our Charming Little Princess
MINA RUTH

No ultrasounds, no genetic testing, Judith was put into a twilight sleep for the birth and first met Mina after she had been washed, wrapped in a fuzzy pink blanket, and adorned with a plastic ankle bracelet. Mina had been given her first bottle by a nurse. The night before, in the snow, Judith had insisted on walking in Central Park, insisted that she couldn't really be in labor yet. After so many years, so many miscarriages, she couldn't believe she was really about to become a mother. All the tiny white shirts, and white cotton mitts to keep the baby from scratching itself, and white baby blankets crocheted by her aunts, must be lying. The insistent pain in her belly and back, the pain that rolled in and withdrew again, must be lying.

January 29, 1965

4:33 a.m.

7 pounds, 4 ounces

21 inches

Parents are requested to examine this report carefully, sign it, and return it promptly. If it is unsatisfactory in any way, a conference with the teacher or principal is advised.

SUBJECTS	Final Average
Arithmetic	B
Civics	B
Cooking	C
Drawing	C
English	B
Geography	A
History	A
Hygiene	A
Music	A
Penmanship	C
Phys. Ed.	A
Reading	A
Science	C
Sewing	B
Spelling	C
Days Absent	0

Proud Parents
Bernard and Judith Cooperman

I married the Defendant on May 15, 1955, in the City of New York, County of New York, State of New York.

How Mina's parents loved her! During her Little Red Riding Hood phase, her father had sewn a clumsy felt cape for her favorite doll when he couldn't find one in a store, and he'd tossed her in the air when she graduated from kindergarten. He had paid for ballet lessons and piano lessons, bought skis and ice skates, wondering which of these skills would stick. Her mother had painted her toenails, read to her, braided her hair (always too tight, but it looked beautiful), allowed her to date whomever, whenever, sent her off to college with a trousseau fit for a royal bride. In 1983, she was the only girl in the dorms with monogrammed towels and sheets, the only one whose mother had sent her on the *train* to Chicago, brought her to Grand Central Station and hired a porter to take her trunk, then led her on board, shoving a pair of new white gloves into her hand. Mina eyed the punks on the next platform jealously, with their spiked hair and thick-soled black boots.

SUPREME COURT OF THE STATE OF NEW YORK
COUNTY OF NEW YORK

Judith Rachel Cooperman, Plaintiff

—against—   **JUDGMENT OF DIVORCE**

Bernard David Cooperman, Defendant

Now on motion of Judith Cooperman, Plaintiff, it is:
ORDERED AND ADJUDGED that the marriage between Judith Cooperman, Plaintiff, and Bernard Cooperman, Defendant, is hereby dissolved by reason of the commission of an act of adultery by Defendant, pursuant to DRL §170(4); and it is further . . .

Dated: June 12, 1985

                              ENTERED:

                                        Robert Gregson
                                        J.S.C.

Last call for Amtrak train number forty, the Broadway Limited: Philadelphia; Harrisburg; Pittsburgh; Akron, Ohio; Cleveland; Toledo; South Bend, Indiana; Chicago, Illinois. Last call. Track Forty-four.

Regular attendance is absolutely necessary for the satisfactory progress of the pupil. Nothing hinders success in school more than irregular attendance. Pupils should learn to be regular and prompt. The Home can help much in the formation of such habits by discouraging unnecessary absence and tardiness.

BURGLARY/VANDALISM: A known female entered her ex-boyfriend's home in the 100 block of Enchanted Hills Road early Tuesday, May 15, 1985, while he was not home and destroyed several pieces of furniture and poured liquid bleach onto his clothing.

DISORDERLY CONDUCT: Mina R. Cooperman, 19, of Chicago, was charged with disorderly conduct after refusing to leave Club 390, 390 E. Joe Orr Road.

ORNAMENTS STOLEN: Two ceramic lawn ornaments were stolen August 23 or 24, 1986, from a home's front yard at 33 The Maples.

SUPREME COURT OF THE STATE OF NEW YORK
COUNTY OF NEW YORK

Judith Rachel Cooperman, Plaintiff

—against—   **AFFIDAVIT OF PLAINTIFF**

Bernard David Cooperman, Defendant

The grounds for dissolution of the marriage are as follows:
Adultery (DRL §170(4)):
That on March 23, 1984, at the premises located at 106 East 86 Street, New York, New York, 10028, the Defendant engaged in sexual intercourse with Moira Rubin, without the procurement nor the connivance of the Plaintiff, and the Plaintiff ceased to cohabit with the Defendant upon the discovery of the adultery. Attached please find the corroborating affidavit of a third-party witness, namely, Mina Ruth Cooperman.

WHEREFORE, I Judith Rachel Cooperman, respectfully request that judgment be entered for the relief sought and for such other relief as the court deems fitting and proper.

Dated: August 16, 1984

Traits

Gives best efforts	+
Accurate	+
Obeys promptly	−
Cheerful	−
Reads between the lines	+
On time with work	−
Concentrates well	+
Uses time wisely	−
Cooperates well	I
Is sneaky	I
Is courteous & kind	I
Avoids quarreling	−
Keeps rules of school	I
Has an obsessive concern for justice	+
Is dependable	I
Shows initiative	+

(+) Strong (−) Needs Improvement (I) Improved

The Plaintiff's address is 106 East 86 Street, New York, New York, 10028. The Defendant's address is 33 The Maples, Roslyn, New York 11576.

SUMMER SHORTS

Although these three short plays are short on style, "The Professor's Parrot" cleanses the palate delightfully between the more somber and plodding works performed on either side of it— "Morning in Michigan" and "The Funeral." In just one act each, these attempt unsuccessfully to delve into the secrets of birth and death, but in striving for less, "The Professor's Parrot" accomplishes more. Especially powerful as Mrs. P is Mina Cooperman who imbues her slight role of the Professor's long-suffering wife with genuine distress as she watches a bird replace her in her husband's affections.

Reviewed by . . . , Special to the *New York Times*
Thursday, October 25, 1990

MINA COOPERMAN AND DANIEL ROZEN

Mina Ruth Cooperman and Daniel Rozen were married Monday evening, June 20, 1998, at the Players Club on Gramercy Park.

The bride, 33, is an actress, most recently seen in the Roundabout Theater Company's production of *The Women*. For the past five seasons, she has been a member of the Oregon Shakespeare Festival in Ashland, Oregon. She graduated from Northwestern University's Theater Department and is the daughter of Judith Cooperman of New York City, and Bernard Cooperman, the prominent trial lawyer, of Roslyn, New York.

The bridegroom, 35, is an independent set designer. He graduated from Pratt Institute. He is the son of Diane Smith of Englewood, N.J., and the late David Rozen.

As children, Mr. Rozen and Ms. Cooperman attended the same summer theater camp, where he remembers her flubbing her lines in the season-ending production of *Romeo and Juliet* and she remembers him dropping a chair just offstage during her big scene.

Mr. Rozen and Ms. Cooperman did not meet again until nearly two decades later when they ran into each other at the premier of a mutual friend's play. She didn't immediately recognize the clean-cut Mr. Rozen. "He used to have really long, wild hair," Ms. Cooperman recalled. Mr. Rozen didn't recognize her either, but once reintroduced, they seemed to see each other everywhere. And, as they say, the rest is history.

At the ceremony, the bride wore a gown modeled on Katherine Hepburn's wedding dress in *Philadelphia Story*. The bridesmaids wore vintage tea dresses and carried bouquets of yellow rosebuds. The groom and ushers wore navy blue.

Over a slice of cake decorated with fresh violets and gold leaf, the bride's father, Bernard Cooperman, noted, "Nothing is too good for my little princess. She's finally getting married."

"She'll be a little bean," Mina was thinking as the technician got the ultrasound machine ready. "I'll see her all curled up and they'll take photos I can take home and show to Dan." She was sure it would be a girl, though she didn't know how she knew. The technician asked if she wanted to know the baby's gender—of course she did—although you can't always see on these tests, it all depends on how the baby's turned. She felt the warm gel spread on her stomach—hated the cute way the tech called it her "tummy" as if she herself were a baby—and imagined her little girl snug against her chest in a BabyBjörn as she walked the length of a train car, traveling from one acting job to another, or sleeping in a playpen backstage, or later reading a picture book while Mina studied her lines. But then the tech was saying, "Hum, just a minute. Let me just come over here," and it seemed to be taking so long that Mina started to worry, first just a slippery feeling in her throat but then her feet turned ice cold and her hands started to shake. "Is there something wrong?" she managed to ask through clenched teeth. "No, no, not at all," the tech said and spun the screen around. "It's twins! See, here. Twin boys. Congratulations!" And that's when Mina screamed.

Having come in, the angel Gabriel said to her, "Rejoice, you highly favored one! Blessed are you among women!" But when she saw him, she was greatly troubled at the saying, and considered what kind of salutation this might be.

But what if it's all a mistake and I'm really him instead of me? We were identical so it's possible, isn't it? That they should have given me the other name when I came out?

Dear Mina and Daniel:

This letter is to confirm our telephone conversation with you that the karyotypic analysis of the fetal cells from the amniotic fluid shows your fetuses to be 46, XY, chromosomally normal monozygotic males. The alpha-fetoprotein was within the normal range, indicating the fetuses probably do not have open neural tube defects. As we discussed, your screening tests for Tay-Sachs disease both showed normal hexosaminidase A enzyme activity levels, indicating their neither of you are carriers for a Tay-Sachs gene.

It was a pleasure to meet you. We are happy the results of your tests are normal and extend our best wishes for the future to you all.

L. Simmer, MD
Attending Physician, Department of Obstetrics and Gynecology
February 25, 2003

OBITUARY

Paul Rozen, infant son of Daniel and Mina Rozen, stillborn on June 20, 2003. Although he never spent any time with us, he touched many of our lives. Survivors include his parents, twin brother Luke, maternal grandparents Judith and Bernard Cooperman, step-grandmother Moira Cooperman, and paternal grandmother Diane Smith.

THE CLASSES—1987—20TH REUNION YEAR!

Ran into *Mina Cooperman* at the premier of *Josh Green's* new play last week. She lives in Manhattan with her husband Daniel Rozen and their four-year-old son, and currently trains sales reps in Pfizer's international division. "I get to pretend I'm a doctor in Paris or Calcutta, while the reps practice selling me the newest drug." She said it's a far cry from playing Hedda Gabler and she'd love any leads!

identity is "a subjective sense as well as an observable quality of personal sameness and continuity, paired with some belief in the sameness and continuity of some shared world image. As a quality of unself-conscious living . . ." Erik Erikson

Not herself but like whom then? No one else but her there with the bleach, with the glass tossed in the guy's face and then one onto the sidewalk, with the stolen gnome and deer. Those had been hard to wrestle into the car, also taken without asking, though her father hadn't reported that theft. He knew she had a key, knew she had to have filched it. He really hadn't known until later that she'd taken the statues—if you could call them that, she thought with a laugh. Moira must have picked them out. Years later, at her wedding, her father had raised his glass to her new husband. She's all yours now, he'd said. Good luck. Ah, she thought, her old weird self had never been forgiven or forgotten.

AN EXODUS FROM BROADWAY, OFF-BROADWAY AND OFF-OFF-BROADWAY

Three dozen theaters go dark as recession brings the curtains down.

By Norm Arnoldson

Friday, December 12, 2008

When the leads come, she doesn't follow.

The captain has illuminated the fasten seatbelt sign. Please return to your seats and make sure that your seatbelts are tightly fastened. As you can tell, we have entered an area of turbulence. If you are sitting next to a loved one, this would be a good time to hold his or her hand. We'll be landing shortly.

NOTICE TO QUIT

To: Daniel Rozen and Mina Cooperman (tenants)
        365 East 7th Street, Apt. 5,
        New York, NY 10009

You are notified that you owe rent in the amount of $7824.00.
If you do not pay this rent by the date stated below, your tenancy is terminated and you must move.
Date and time by which rent must be paid: Date: October 23, 2008.
Time: 10:00 a.m.
If you pay your rent in full before this date and time, you do not have to move.
If you do not pay your rent or move by this date and time, a lawsuit may be filed to evict you.

Date: October 16, 2008   Signature: _____

```
┌─────────────────────────────────────────────────────────────┐
│               LANDLORD'S RECORD OF SERVICE                   │
│                                                               │
│  On October 16, 2008 at 10 a.m:                              │
│                                                               │
│    X  I attempted to make personal service on the tenants    │
│       named above. I knocked on the door of the premises,    │
│       and no one answered. Although I heard voices and       │
│       other noises from inside, I believed tenants were      │
│       absent, having mistakenly left a television on when    │
│       they went out, and so I securely affixed this Notice   │
│       to the entry door of the above premises.               │
│                                                               │
│  October 16, 2008        _____ │
│       Date                            Signature              │
└─────────────────────────────────────────────────────────────┘
```

What if my old room was really his room and he's there now? Maybe that's why we needed to move.

When Mom told me I had a twin who died, I thought how happy I was I didn't have to share my room with him because it's really small, just big enough for my bed and dresser and a place on the floor to play. And now I have to share a room at Granddad's instead, which is even worse, and almost all my stuff's in boxes. Mom and me (and Dad when he's here) sleep in the den, since the bedrooms are full of my uncles—uncles!—even though they're practically young enough to be my brothers. The one called Saul teases me all the time about my fire helmet. A fireman gave it to me, but here we drive to school in the morning and there's no fire station to walk by or firemen to wave to on the way. Sometimes I say something about missing home and Dad, but then I see how sad Mom is and I remember to shut up.

Maybe he is me—or was me. My twin, I mean. But if there's only one of us, it has to be me—doesn't it? I can't be him. Or can I? What if he's really inside me? How would I even know him if I met him? I guess he'd look like me, but probably not exactly alike because Sharon and Ruth at school are identical twins and I can tell them apart. Maybe it doesn't really matter if I'm him instead of me, because we'd turn out to be the same anyway, but I'd say that's not really true, because we wouldn't end up being exactly the same, even if we were identical. Maybe all this time, I thought I was me but I was supposed to be the one to die. Maybe I did die and I've been him all along without even knowing it.

The Plaintiff's address was 106 East 86 Street, New York, New York, 10028. The Plaintiff's address was 365 East 7th Street, Apt. 5, New York, NY 10009. The Defendant's address was 33 The Maples, Roslyn, New York 11576. The Defendant's address is unknown.

ORDERED AND ADJUDGED that both parties are authorized to resume the use of any former surname, and it is further

Disintegration

I'm ashamed when I need to ask a question again or things slip my mind—Mina's birthday, for example—and so I make excuses: "I was so busy with my book group that I forgot your present" or "What was that? The radio's so loud," for example, and then I fret—where has the time gone? What about the things I've lost?

Mina stood at the window, watching the cars down on Central Park West fifteen stories below. They looked like the colorful beads on the wire sculpture at the pediatrician's office, a series of swirls along which Luke's fingers pushed a blue bead, then a red, then a green. At the top of a peak, he let them rattle back to the sculpture's base. When her mother's yellow taxi pulled up below, bringing her back from three weeks in Europe, Mina's shoulders tensed. Danny had taken Luke to pick her up at the airport, while Mina straightened the apartment and went grocery shopping and made dinner. By rights Mina should have been the one to meet her mother, but the apartment had been a chaos that Danny wouldn't have known how to start cleaning. Mina still couldn't quite tell if the mess had been longstanding or just the detritus of packing and then the dust of the few weeks' vacation.

Some days, I find the bathroom and kitchen harder to find, the laundry harder to fold, my keys harder to clean, but then I find them in an old coat pocket and everything's OK.

First her mother got out of the taxi, then Luke tumbled out onto all fours, wagging his tush and nodding his head—a horse maybe? Or a dog? At home they always had a bowl of water on the kitchen floor just waiting for their son/pet to lap up. Then, after a pause during which Danny presumably paid the fare, her husband emerged and went round to the trunk to get Judith's suitcase.

The teacup was safely in Mina's handbag, wrapped in a wad of paper towels, her grandmother's teacup, the one with purple roses around the rim and solid gold inside. As a child, Mina had imagined this teacup had mates somewhere, and saucers, and bowls for strawberries and cream, and gold-plated teaspoons, and a whole castle to go with it. On the drowsy winter weekends when she'd been left at her Baba's, she had peered into its sunny depths. She hadn't seen it for years, but she'd found it today, shoved to the back of the top shelf of a kitchen cabinet. It was clear that her mother no longer prized the thing, perhaps didn't even remember it.

Judith rarely cooks any longer. In the kitchen, she mistakes salt for sugar, burns the peas and throws them out, eats only ladyfinger cookies for supper. But she takes her aide to hear the philharmonic, and after the concert, in the taxi, they discuss the Bartok versus the Beethoven, and whether the new, young first cello, with the mop of blond hair, is up to the task.

Suddenly, in the middle of dinner, after the story about visiting Mozart's house in Salzburg and before the story about running into a childhood friend in Budapest, Judith said, "Look what I found!" She went swiftly into the other room and came back with something flat wrapped in brown paper. Mina's thoughts drifted to Julie Andrews— brown paper packages wrapped up with string. Inside the package was a saucer, with purple roses around its rim and a circle of solid gold in the center, upon which a teacup could perfectly rest. Mina almost said: "How funny! I just stole that teacup and here you come with a matching saucer!" She was still pondering what she should actually say when her mother got up and headed straight for the kitchen cupboard.

"Mom!" she called. "Mom, I broke it."

At dinner before the concert, Judith tries to sip her wine through the lemon wedge garnishing her water glass.
The aide must tell the driver where Judith lives and carry Judith's keys.

"When? Today?"

At the museum she leans on her walker and speaks to the Matisse as if the painting is her old friend.

"No, no. A long time ago." In her handbag, the hottest kiln ever, the fires of hell are turning the precious cup to ash. "When you were in the hospital. I was cleaning . . ."

For the last time, Judith thinks how all days are the same, able to distinguish "same" and "days," before she nods off again.

Her mother had come back to stand in the doorway. Now she sat down heavily, and Danny shot Mina a weird look.

"I'm sorry. I didn't know it mattered," Mina said.

"It was the only thing of my mother's . . . Well, I loved it when I was little. The only nice thing we had. I couldn't bear to use it without the saucer though, and then in Budapest we found one. In an antique shop."

She can shuffle along, holding on to someone's shoulders, being told "Lift your feet! Lift your feet!"
The doctor says that Ritalin will keep her more alert.

In bed that night, Danny will say, "I thought you were going to blame Luke. Say that he broke it," and Mina will feel outraged that he thinks her capable of such a thing, forgetting that she had done something perhaps even more reprehensible. Now, she cringed, anticipated . . . , until her mother laughed. And patted her hand.

At first she responds to stimuli more readily, but the following weeks show a return to somnolence. The dosage must be increased.

"I broke the saucer when I was packing her things, after she died," Judith said. "Remember that tile counter she had down in Miami Beach? It just slipped from my hands and—*poof*—it was gone! Smithereens."

Mina had been afraid her mother would forget her passport or miss her plane—but she remembered this.

"Why didn't you tell me?"

She spends hours watching shadows cross the corners of the room.
Her hands remember knitting, the same pink scarf for weeks.

Mina remembered the tile counter too—aqua blue—and the beach that smelled of Coppertone and the red vinyl bikini she had talked her mother into buying for her and the ladies wearing mink stoles in the lobbies of the fancy hotels no matter how hot it was outside. In her mind, she could return to all those things, and in the future, by speaking of them, she will be able to return them to her mother too, in the manner of gifts. There will be things she won't remind her mother of, gifts of the over-and-done-with, gifts of allowing her to forget. For example, did her mother remember drowning the kittens? Something Mina had thought she would never forgive her for, tossed into the sea in a bag on a rainy night, but it turns out to be of questionable importance.

When asked what they should discuss, Judith says, "Nice things."
But Mina wonders, does she know what that means?

It seemed impossible for Mina to return the teacup. If only she could reel time back in! Instead, it moved inexorably forward.

My Mina, my Luke, miss you now always.

Mina wouldn't be able to use the teacup for years, until this evening was lost to Judith and Daniel and even Luke, who now lifted his head from his ice cream and stared at her, licking his spoon and clutching the painted glass elk his grandmother had brought back for him, its antlers fine as needles. Was even he waiting for her to say something?

She finds talking on the phone nearly impossible.
For visitors, she opens her eyes.
She still likes to sing, claps joyously at pictures of dogs.

The teacup will need to be buried behind dishware Mina never uses, perhaps even until after her mother dies. Then Mina will pull it out again—or rediscover it, if she herself has forgotten it by then—the only thing.

Now swallowing becomes difficult.
Stare without seeing.
TV on.
Sleep.

Looking at her family, Mina imagined the teacup languishing behind the Thanksgiving gravy boat, and thought, "No. I'll let Luke play with it, or lap milk from it. I'll even let him break it."

Visitation

In the cluttered living room, Mina finds it impossible to remove herself from the gaze of her four-year-old, who says, "I'm watching you, Momma," glitter in his eye. The radiator steams with wet socks, and outside, in the dark, snow gathers even at the bottom of the air-shaft their back windows look out on. "Where we going *now?*" he says as Mina gathers up mittens and shoves his arms back into the sleeves of his winter coat, and who can blame him—just returned from preschool and groceries and bank—but she needs to visit her mother, and now is the only time this week she can think to go.

After the subway, at the home, they can tell her mother from the others in the dining room by the tight braid she does herself and then scrolls so neatly into a bun that Mina needs to remember why her mother's here every time she sees it. Her son clutches her hand, apprehensive of the folks in wheelchairs—what a cliché, she thinks, maybe he's really afraid of slipping on the highly polished floor or hoping for a taste of the sticky gravy that coats the slices of turkey or a slurp of the sweet and salty apple crisp lying in wait for dessert, and sometimes her mother does feed him her own dinner, one tiny bite at a time off the end of her blunt-tined fork, his mouth always open like a baby bird's, and her Mom going, "Mmmm . . . lunch . . . lunch," as she feeds him. "Mom," she says now, "Mamele," and places her free hand on her mother's shoulder, and her mother turns around, puzzled, and then says, "My, you two are a sight for sore eyes."

Today her son won't let go of her hand so that she can give her mother a hug and she ends up making an awkward gesture that includes both of them, his arm slung around her mother's neck, her mother's breath in both their ears as if . . . They sit down and wait for her to eat, but instead, she watches them, reaching out to stroke one cheek and then another, saying, "It's so cold outside." With the decorations up—nondenominational snowflakes and jolly Santas and blue and silver dreidels—her mother could hardly fail to realize that the holidays are approaching, and she says, "Are you going away this year? Going on vacation?"

Finally her son climbs into Mina's lap, struggles out of his coat, lays his head against her chest, and plays with the buttons on his red plaid shirt, then with the big ones on her sweater front with the whorls he likes to trace, like fingerprints with his fingerprints. She takes the coat, sticks it into the tote she's carrying, already full of crayons and markers, pages from coloring books copied on her office machine, stickers, toy trucks and trains, bendy pipe cleaners and a deck of cards, snack crackers filled with cheese, apple juice in a box. Her mother starts the conversation, the only conversation, and while Mina tells her again where they've been and how they've been and what her eynikl wants for Chanukah and where they're going for vacation, she notices the boy's eyes start to drift closed—it must be the heat in here, kept so that the old folks can wear their summer clothes all year round—but then he opens one with a pop and says, "I've got my eye on you!" and giggles.

Later, when she gets up to use the bathroom, he follows her—down the hall, through the door, into the stall, where he plays with the lock while she pees, and asks, "What's that for?" pointing to the paper seat covers and the tampon dispenser, and after she names them, asks again, "But what's it *for?*" and Mina just doesn't answer because those are two topics she really doesn't want to get into right now—disease and menstruation. When they get back to the dining room, they find that the meal is over and her mother has been moved back to her room, shepherded more like, the aides as tenacious as sheepdogs shuffling the residents along. Her mother is sitting on the side of her bed, tangled in the sleeves of her nightie although it's only six-thirty, and once they finally get her head through the top, she looks at them, startled, and says, "Oh, you're here. Where have you been? But you have your coats on. Are you going away? Where are you going?"

Mina sits down on her mother's bed, so narrow, confined by bars, and "We'll be back," she says—tries to say—as comfortably as possible.

Her son has snuggled in between her legs, pushing her up tight against her mother so that her mother nearly topples, and he takes his hand, which he's somehow managed to get into his mitten, and rubs Mina's tummy and looks up at her with sheep's eyes, pulls her head down toward his and whispers, "I'm watching you," and then licks her ear. Now he's kneeling, slid down to the tile, pressing his head up against her crotch as if he's trying to get back in, as if the umbilical cord had never been cut. Between their two hot bodies, Mina can't breathe, and she reaches to push his inappropriate—that's the word she always uses when he does this—head away, and her mother suddenly leans against her even more fiercely and asks again, "Where are you going?"

On Seeing the Skeleton of a Whale
in the Harvard Museum
of Natural History

Mina stood on the museum balcony and looked down at the sperm whale's skeleton and at the whale's great lidless skull suspended above the taxidermied mammals, stiff in their splitting skins. Outside, over Cambridge, across the river and out over Boston harbor, clouds spattered rain; inside, dust settled on the wooden floor, the vitrine holding two hundred species of hummingbird, all these bones of old things, and her son Luke beside her, his fleshy hand on the railing. From a plaque he read aloud how the sperm whale had been prized especially for the waxy-white substance in its case—No, not a suitcase, Mom (Luke was a great joker), the whole top of its huge square head—which was used to make the finest candles in New England, and fine lubricants of all sorts: watch oil, transmission fluid, grease for lenses and delicate high-altitude instruments. Its blubber, boiled down, ignited the streetlamps of London, and ambergris from its intestine stabilized the perfumes of France. From other whales the great curtains of baleen, cut from the mouth, fashioned corset stays, he read, and poked her side where a corset might have hugged her.

Behind them, her father sat on a bench, tapping his cane in an indecipherable rhythm. She'd come to Boston for him, mostly, to decide what to do. He'd taken a position at the law school, moved with her stepmother, and then she had gone, died a few years before. Now he can't live alone. He refuses to do anything but live alone. At the museum entrance, they'd run into one of his former students—obsequious, shining, clearly forgotten—who had grasped her father's hands with pleasure, and Mina had thought for a second of hiring him—or someone like him . . . It didn't seem possible to decide what to do.

She felt as if she were looking down through the seaweed-clenched water near a pier. Around her: air, no other human. She could see the whale's long, narrow bottom jaw with its ten-inch conical teeth and its top jaw too, its strong naked spine, and its flippers whose bones looked just like those in her hands. More than anything, the flipper hands convinced her the whale was indeed a mammal, more than its warm blood, more than its need to breathe air, more than its nursing of young. For two years or more, it nursed its young.

The jaw was clear, but where was the top of the skull? she wondered. Gone. An emptiness. The day she gave birth to her son, her father had his first stroke. "Is he diminished?" a friend had asked.

There go flukes. Chimney's afire. The bloody spout of a wounded whale.

Around the balcony, etchings in frames—she showed Luke pictures of men at both ends of the whaling journey: hoisting the sails, then standing inside beached whale ribcages that soared up around them like cathedral doorways. Boys not much older than he peeled off the sheets of blubber in a spiral, like ton-weight skins of orange, and the whale's carcass turned and turned until it dropped into the sea.

The strokes kept coming. Each time she'd been fooled into thinking that her father would recover. Instead, he'd slipped further away until the cumulative effect was a silence cleansed of memory and all but the simplest language. "My turkey?" he said after the most recent stroke, motioning to shave himself. In the center of his brain now, one would find a puddle of blood.

Next, pictures of all-hands-on-deck, ready to lower the whaleboats, a boatsteerer with his harpoon at the ready. Sometimes the whalers would wound a calf, knowing its blood would bring the mother round. The clicks with which cow and calf called each other—a sort of song?— could stun a man underwater, the sound not a sound at all but a knock to the chest. "You fools," Mina thought. "You thought your fate was separate from the fate of the whale."

"I'll bring grandpa over," Luke said. He went and extended his hand.

She watched the anger rise like a wave in her father's face. "I won't," he said. "I won't," and raised his cane, waving it so that her son backed away. "You better do something about that boy," her father called after, then uttered a series of curses loud enough to echo.

"Yeah, Mr. No Memory," Luke muttered. The day before, he'd made faces behind her father's back, mimicked his halting speech, and stuck his foot out, right where her father's cane was heading. She'd seen the scared look in her father's watery blue eyes. And then the day before that, it had been her father's cane sticking out at the top of the stairs, right where Luke was heading. They made a fine pair.

"You go to him, Mom."

Oh, there have been times she wanted to do the same—stick her foot right out—and times she was the foot, stuck everywhere, but just the week before, her father had fallen outside a yoga studio, and when the teacher and all the students went to rescue him, he hadn't known where he was. At home, she and Luke had left plants unwatered, clean clothes in a messy pile, a cat the neighbors had promised to feed. All these would need tending to.

"No," she said. "No. He's fine there. He's perfectly happy. Let him just sit there." She smiled at her father and waved stupidly.

Sometimes the whalemen slipped in blood and oil on the ship's deck and slid into the ocean for sharks to eat. Sometimes a hand might reach for them.

Behold them in the gathering dusk, with a whale roped to either side of the ship.

"My father's already gone," she thought, "left this land for sea." Then, "Sing," she demanded, kneeling before him. "Teach my son to whistle, dammit." And her father pursed his lips, but she didn't think it was in a whistling shape. Was he trying? Was he making fun? He'd been a great tease, the snowballs just missing her face.

In the car up from New York, she and Luke had been singing a lot of sea chanteys. "Heave away, haul away," they sang and "Farewell to Nova Scotia, ye sea bound coast. May your mountains dark and dreary be," but when she asked her father to sing one of the old ones for her, "Shenandoah" or "Deep Blue Sea," he couldn't remember them, although he'd sung their refrains to her maybe a million times. "Oh, you pinks and posies. Go down, you blood-red roses. Go down," she sang instead.

After they'd been thrice around the balcony, learning about the killing and processing of whales, she took Luke's hand and left her father behind, sitting on the bench, her little white-haired father with his dapper white goatee, his cheeks as soft as a series of clichés. Her son played with her fingers, although he hadn't let me hold his hand since he was six, and they went outside, and a feeling of buoyancy overtook her.

Luke began to sing, first softly and then loudly since they weren't in the museum anymore: "All for me grog, me jolly jolly grog, all for me beer and tobacco. I spent all me tin on the lassies drinking gin, and it's o'er the western oceans I must wander."

And she laughed and laughed to hear her eleven-year-old sing that with such feeling and he laughed too, because he knew it was funny— that jokester.

Blood was thicker, they always said, but maybe it wasn't. Or maybe only some blood. She turned to Luke and watched his face as he stepped into the light, a curtain lifting. And they walked away.

Causes of death: food poisoning, massive waves, illness, fighting, infected wounds, whales, the ice-cold sea.

Later, years later, long after her father is dead and she has tossed his ashes into the ocean off Maine, Mina will think back on this afternoon and her stomach will turn again and again like the phrase in a song. She can't let go of it—how monstrous she'd been, how foolish, how she left her father there on the dusty bench, his hands clutching the cane and his mouth waiting to smile again at their return, at these two faces he still recognized. Because she has seen the skeleton again and realized that the top of its skull *is* there, the sleigh, the chariot, the coach, the whale-men called it: a small space for the brain to tuck inside. The skull houses the brain and the brain its secrets, even her father's brain—perhaps, perhaps—though his eyes were dim and liquid.

Princess of Desire

I was merely his customer: that's what she said. Although she had briefly fantasized that a baby girl could sleep through rehearsals in a Moses basket or later, color or read books while she learned her lines, she had finally set aside any thought of having a husband or family and instead traveled as an actress. She bought carpets, like the Pakistani one on her table that she rubbed, her palm on its fine nub, and she'd taken lovers. Now she faced the policeman, a silver letter opener spinning over and over and over in her hand, and answered his questions.

For many years, she'd had a crush on a merchant in her town, a seller of carpets, and so her home was filled with carpets: carpets covered her tables as well as her floors, and when the soft spring light came through a window, she sat at one of these tables and imagined he would walk through the door and she'd turn her head and the light would glance off her pearl earring. When she was home, she went to the market every Saturday to see him, this rather rotund fellow with a tendency to light one cigarette from the stub of the last and to blow his nose into a large handkerchief—nothing glamorous about him and no way to explain the attraction but there it was. Her informers had informed her that he was happily married to his childhood sweetheart and that together they'd had ten children. Perhaps his happy marriage and love of his family—whose pictures adorned his market stall—was part of his appeal? Still, she did try to break that marriage apart, to dent it, to bend him. First she wore a tight dress of pale blue silk, then she wore a dress of silver brocade, and finally a golden dress embroidered with all the colors of the rainbow that she thought he'd especially like—his carpets were so colorful. Each time, she'd spent half an hour settling her breasts into the cups of her brassiere perfectly so, and each time he rejected her—gently—but still he tossed her back the way a wise fisherman tosses back a fish that's too small and forgot about her. Although she had done all this, although she tucked her feet into carpet slippers when she came home and she packed a carpet bag when she left again, although she saved the softest carpets to cover her bed, she was merely his customer—that's what she said.

Of course she had other lovers. She was shy around the rug merchant but not around other men. Different towns, different lovers, but after her own lightning bolt of orgasm she was bored. She knew she should try to please them as much as they had pleased her, but instead, staring at the ceiling or the wall or the pillow, she tried to make as many different words out of the word "boredom" as she could. Bedroom, of course, and bed and rod and do, as in "do her." Then bore, as in "bore into her," bore out the ore, as well as bore her, here in her dorm where she roomed with the other actresses, deep in their REM sleep. No true Romeo, no white robe, no church dome, no oboe music. No doe, she, producing no roe, no brood to brood over. Just this mode of being, this demo she's doomed to redo. Another boor to deal out the cards for ombre, pick more brome grass for, visit the rodeo with, use the broom to straighten the room, hope she's not booed off the stage or out of bed. If she'd had that baby girl she'd fantasized about, she'd be sleeping now in the Moses basket beneath the window or sitting in the dining hall downstairs filling the pages of a coloring book, and she imagined that after the man left her, she could turn to the child's special sweet warmth, but she had set aside any thought of having a husband or family and instead traveled as an actress.

She worked in one town or another, three months here, a month there, sometimes just a week or two of work with a hiatus at home in between. She started out playing Mary in the local Passion Play (not the Virgin but the other one), then Ophelia (but not for her the mad maiden), Viola and Rosalynd, Cordelia (that ornery queen), and then broadened her roles from Shakespeare to Ibsen to Brecht—the farces, the musicals, and the epics. City to city, she played Nora and Hedda Gabler, the bride in *A Respectable Wedding*, both the Fly and Lilian in *Happy End*, and Kattrin, the mute daughter in *Mother Courage*. She imagined that one day she'd play Mother Courage herself. Finally she joined a repertory company in a city far from home—a whole year's contract—and was playing Lady MacBeth for the first time when she met a man who interested her more than the others. While learning her lines, she thought of the rug merchant and his wife and whether their relationship was as passionate as the relationship between MacBeth and his wife, but the young man she'd started seeing made these thoughts less urgent than they had been. At least he distracted her more than other lovers had. His appeal lay in his jolliness, in the cleanliness of everything he touched, and in certain bedroom techniques I won't describe. He was a manufacturer and purveyor of pickles—sweet and sour, garlic and dill, fruit and vegetable—and his great and serious knowledge of them amused her no end. It amused her no end that she was spending time with a pickle merchant—the affair couldn't possibly be serious. He even imported pickled eggs from the far off Far East, though after tasting one, she couldn't imagine who would actually buy the things in this provincial town. She humored him though, tasting each of his wares and telling him exactly what to say to make them more enticing to his female customers. She found that between performances, she liked best to settle on a stool in the back of his shop, his realm, and watch him turn the jars on his shelves just this way, just that way, so that the pickles inside—the dark green cornichon, the light green watermelon rind, the purple beets and plums, the yellowish asparagus—all caught the light. The way he rubbed his rotund stomach reminded her of something though she couldn't say what. She spent so much time with him, in the shop during the mornings and in his home after her performances at night, that he began to speak of their future together—forgetting that she would be leaving town at the end of the season. He spoke of the children they might have—jokingly at first, asking if they might be weaned straight from the breast to pickle juice. She laughed weakly at these jokes, for she was nowhere near as young as he thought, and it seemed unlikely that she'd ever have a baby. Still, she didn't dissuade him of his ideas, merely hoped that she would lose interest in him and he in her before she needed to turn down a proposal. But then he began to call her princess, because of the golden ribbon she sometimes wore in her hair and the straight seat she took on the stool, and she found herself succumbing. At home she had constantly bought carpets, because she never tired of visiting the merchant's market stall and listening to him discuss warp, weft, woof, knots per inch, and patterns. She had bought carpets from Spain, Persia, New Mexico, and India and had dreamed of traveling to those places with him—or really of his discovering her in a theater in one of those distant places when he arrived to acquire more carpets, but it had been a long time now since she'd bought carpets or considered other lovers. He was joking—or was he joking—when he told her that if she stayed she'd be a princess?

One afternoon as she sat in the back of the shop, happy to be out of the rain, happy to have an hour off between rehearsal and performance, his cell phone rang and out he went, reminding her to mind the store as if she were already its mistress. At first there was a steady stream of lady customers, eager to buy the last side dish to go with their dinners, and then a steady stream of gentleman customers, eager for something sour to cut the greasy fish and chips they'd bought in the shop next door. Soon, though, the customers stopped coming, and it was almost time for her own light dinner before heading to the theater, and she wondered where her man had gone. In the manner of all stories, the surprising information came as a surprise. As she pulled cheese and crackers from her bag and ate them with pickles, she flipped through his desk calendar, or the mailman walked in with a letter she needed to sign for, or a fairy disguised as an old hag came in and told her—out of the blue—or a pickle jar broke and she needed to retrieve sponge and mop and cleaning fluid from under the sink where she discovered some papers. Just then, the jar slipped from her hand, a shatter of glass, a scatter of pickles, brine everywhere! Under the sink, she finds carpet samples, the carpet merchant's name and address, a birthday card addressed to her man and signed "love, Dad." I know you don't believe this—that after traveling miles from home, she's taken up with the son of her old crush—but stranger things happen every day.

She doesn't tell him that she knows his father, and although she tells herself her new knowledge should change nothing, of course it does. Of course it does. At night now, in bed with him, she no longer delights in his vinegary smell because beneath the sour, she thinks she can smell dust, the dust of old carpets and the faraway places where those carpets were woven and even the dust of her closed-up apartment back in the other city, where carpets cover every surface. When he sighs above her, she imagines his father's voice, and her only pleasure comes from imagining that his penis is a puppet and his father's penis is inside it. It all becomes so unbearable that she must leave, but she returns, and when she does, he tells her that his father is dead. He's only just heard. The police think it's suspicious. She faces him now, the policeman, a silver letter opener spinning over and over and over in her hand.

There were more receipts from you than from any other single person, the policeman says. Yes, she says, I know. Numerous times the policeman comes, and she answers his questions the same way each time. I wasn't a real ruler, she insists, not even a real princess, just the princess of desire—or was it prisoner? I was merely his customer.

Bad Mother

A Story in Five Paragraphs

Once there was a woman with four children under the age of ten: two boys, two girls; two blond, two dark; two boisterous, two subdued. When the eldest complained that she loved him the least, she said, "No, no. That's not true, and besides, I loved you first," which satisfied him for a while. Sometimes she could hear him not quite repeating her words, gloating to himself or to his siblings, "Momma loves me first." When her younger sister asked her which child she loved best, she said, "Don't be ridiculous! I love them all the same, just as our mother loved us the same," even though she knew that their mother had *not* loved them the same. On her deathbed, their mother had pulled her close, hand on her shirtfront surprisingly strong. "I always loved you best. Remember that," she whispered like a threat. On sunny days when one child suddenly broke the family's harmony, she told herself, "I don't love one more than another. I just love them differently." But this was a lie. All of it was a lie. She did love one best, and not the baby as you might expect, but the second eldest, a boy whose greatest pleasure, it seemed, was to slip his hand into hers then quickly out again, and leave something behind in her palm. She loved him better than all the others.

She loved him better than her oldest son. Her best friend, who had only one child, said, "I didn't have another because I could never love anyone as much as I love him." She, on the other hand, had had a second child specifically because she loved the first so much. She'd wanted to experience that love again, to feel it multiplied. Then, what a surprise to experience a love even wilder, fiercer, stronger, deeper. Her first child was quietly willful, and brilliant, and totally focused on the task at hand. Told to clean up his room, he put the toys away but then also got out the dust rags, the vacuum, and the Windex. He excelled on tests of all sorts, both physical and academic, but his mother had to admit that while she found his persistence admirable, she found his fastidiousness trying and his need for approval exhausting. Whenever he brought home a report card, he sat on the front stoop until she returned from work and wouldn't let her go inside, despite the December snow or June heat, until she had noted every grade and every glowing comment. Neighbors remarked on how proud she must be, but privately she preferred the second child, whose grades varied—high in the subjects he loved (which changed every year), low in those he had no patience for, whose room always looked like a ransacked casino, and whose favorite phrase, gleaned from a self-help book he'd found on his aunt's bedside table (happy to read that as anything else) was "Sometimes good is good enough." His memory was terrible and his ability to reason logically was limited, but the minute he touched something he thought of a question to ask about it.

She loved this second child better than she loved her third one, too, the one she'd had in an attempt to diffuse the either/or relationship she had with the first two. For a while it worked. It helped that the third was a girl, and that the woman could go out and buy new clothes for her (girl clothes) rather than relying on hand-me-downs, shallow though this might be. This baby destroyed pink though, and knew how to throw herself into a rage for apparently no reason at all. Once she grew teeth, she ate everything: corncobs as well as kernels, chicken bones, her blanket, pages torn from books—like a beautiful goat. For she was such a beautiful child that strangers stared in the grocery store and told her to sign the baby up for a modeling contract, so beautiful that she, herself, couldn't stop looking at the little girl's perfect oval face, her eyes such a light blue they seemed to reflect the sky, her golden curls. The second child had golden curls too, but while the baby's were lovely ringlets, his were disorderly and knotted, frizzy on one side of his head, loosely loopy on the other. And his nose was bulbous, his lips too thin, his large ears stuck out, his neck too long—the kind of child who prompted relatives to remark that true beauty is on the inside. His mother loved his puppy ungainliness but also hoped, for his sake, that he was merely an ugly duckling, destined to grow into a swan.

She loved her second child better than she loved her fourth too, the second girl, called Baby, always the baby, who told funny knock-knock jokes, and was so ticklish that she giggled even before your fingers found the sweet spot on the side of her waist, and laughed at everything, even her siblings' falls and failures—not because she was malicious but because she really and truly saw the humor in everything. She assumed that when they tripped, they did so just to amuse her, and that when they quarreled, it was for her amusement too, like the Punch and Judy show she had seen once on TV. The second child didn't laugh at the comics, could never remember his own punch lines, and looked blank when other people told jokes. "I don't get it," he said until even his kind youngest sister rolled her eyes. "Perhaps his seriousness will lead him to do great things," his mother thought.

She'd planned her children two years apart, and had imagined them as stair-steps, littlest to biggest, youngest to oldest, separate but equal. She had pictured their photos marching tidily up the wall alongside the real steps in her house. In the heart, though, nothing is separate but equal. In fact, she stumbled up, stumbled down, stumbled among her children. Sometimes she wondered if her great love for her second child grew out of pity, or guilt, or the fact that she most closely recognized herself in him. Of course, she hoped that his lack of ambition, timidity, and imperfect sense of humor wouldn't make it difficult for him to find his way in the world! Of course, she worried that she was treating her other children unfairly and hoped she hid this as well as her mother had hidden her own unfair feelings. Of course, she worried that she identified with him too much. She, too, had been dull-witted, unattractive, and clumsy compared to her siblings. All this. But mostly she loved him because he demanded nothing, and her love grew every time his hand slipped into hers, even once he'd become a teenager, grew from the berry he left behind, the bluebird feather, the striped pebble, the coin, the glove she'd dropped two blocks back, a meticulously drawn space-ship on a scrap of old envelope. These things made her long to pet him, his unruly hair, his dirty shirts, his puzzled expression.

Seven Little Stories about 1977

Waves

Waves equal time, and this was a long time ago. Once, back then (seven, seventy-seven), it seemed one wave led to the next and there'd always be another one coming, as Anna's grandfather used to say. But he meant buses or women, and he meant don't get upset, don't freak out, don't stress, don't put all your eggs in one basket, and so on. First she would be a girl and then she would be a woman. She still played with dolls—really, paper dolls that she drew herself, naked (the dolls were naked, not the girl), with perfectly even, round breasts and flat feet, and then drew all the clothes—purple disco suits, bikinis, silver minidresses with fringe, patched and embroidered bell-bottom jeans, and so on—but she knew she would soon outgrow that pastime and find another. She would outgrow reading *The Lord of the Rings* over and over and over, each time she finished starting again so that she could keep living in Middle Earth, and read *Moby Dick* instead (she couldn't imagine going to college without having read *Moby Dick*) and then maybe a psychology textbook. She would be married by twenty-four, have her first child by twenty-eight. She knew these things were coming, wave after wave. But does time really work that way—one moment after another, a sequence of waves? Apparently, it's not true that waves come in sets of seven, with every seventh wave bigger than the rest. And the seventh of the seventh group and so on, bigger and bigger, like the orderly development of a plot. But she thought that way at the time: high school and college and graduate school. A career with steps, too, writing one book and then another bigger and more important book, or dancing for a little modern company in a downtown loft and then at St. Marks and eventually the Joyce Theater, or something helping people—a therapist

111

to children and then teaching others how to befriend and salve. A boyfriend and then a husband and then the father of her kid(s).

She knew the moon pulled the tides back and forth across the world, like a seesaw or a tennis ball across the net. She knew that hair grew back after even the worst haircut. She knew that her skin cells regenerated every twenty-seven days and that her liver could regenerate in four months. A new one like the old one—was there an actual difference?

She failed to see the rocking motion, the slithering, seaweed caught in water, waving at her. Or otters eating clams. They wind themselves in seaweed to sleep, so they don't drift off into deep ocean. She failed to see this too, that this summer was her still spot, tethering her back to safety. She failed to see that after this, in a year, or less, time would bob and weave faster and more erratically, her dinghy wander.

Good Girls

When Anna was seventeen, her parents went to Europe and left her the summerhouse in Maine and the dogs to take care of, a blind and deaf sheepdog who loved to eat paper napkins off of people's laps and a Puli who barked when guests left rather than when they arrived. Both were shaggy and unkempt, and she'd gotten her mother's permission to shave them for the summer. Now they were ugly but happier.

She brought two of her friends from New York with her, Emma and Janice. They read murder mysteries and couldn't figure out where the time went: week passed week passed week. Despite their easy agreements about food, and their similar faded jeans and flowing India-print dresses, they were not actually the same girl. Emma, née Beth (she had renamed herself after Emma Goldman), lived in Queens, rode the subway an hour in each direction to school, figuring math or reading the *New York Times*. She shared the only bedroom with her mother, while her sisters slept on the pull-out couch in the living room, and the desire to leave that apartment behind was like a flame inside her. Later that same summer, she took the Green Tortoise bus to San Francisco, and, when she returned to the city, moved in with their friend Mike who lived with his older brothers in an apartment furnished only with mattresses and stacks of comic books. Anna didn't know if Emma was fucking Mike and wasn't sure if she was jealous—even if Emma wasn't—did that make sense? Janice, an only child, had dinner with her parents every night, holding her mom's hand as they ate. She wore her long hair in two braids, wrote poetry, and played the guitar. Anna's parents mostly just left her alone. Together, the girls had been to the War is Over celebration in Central Park, joined a rally to support the United Farm Workers, traveled to New Haven for a Dylan concert, mourned together the death by suicide of the singer Phil Ochs, held an identical regret that they'd been too young to go to Woodstock. At the protest that Emma organized to support the teacher's strike at their school, Janice handed out leaflets and flowers. No, that wasn't her in the famous photo of a girl putting a flower in the barrel of a gun—that was ten years earlier during a march on the Pentagon—but Anna often thought Janice had modeled herself after that other girl. What had happened to that girl, to her striped shirt and bucket hat?

In Maine, the girls made coffee in the mornings and drank it outside on the stoop. Every afternoon they took the dogs and walked a mile to the pond, swam and sunned naked. The walk back was hot and long—they had to keep waiting for the sheepdog, saying, "Come on, boy. That's a good boy. Come on now," or tunneling into the brush by the side of the road to find the Puli who'd run off while they waited for the sheepdog. They cooked dinner once the house had cooled off, then played cards and listened to LPs on the shoddy stereo and forgot to water the garden. Sometimes, folding a piece of paper over and over, they played Exquisite Corpse, laughing at how their drawings of flowers and cows lined up or didn't, and sometimes they each chose an object, then described it without naming it so that the others needed to guess the special word. Anna wrote this: "Slats faded, nets shreds, demoted to decoration. The owners tried to rid the wood of weeds and bugs by soaking it in ammonia before topping it with a slab of glass and turning it into a coffee table."

She was disappointed when neither of her friends could guess "lobster trap" although they saw them every time they drove into town to buy groceries—stacked next to shacks waiting for the fishermen to take them out and drop them in the water or tacked up decoratively against the side of a rental cottage or turned into the base for a mailbox. She thought it was perhaps the sign that her guests were tired of her, of feeling beholden to her—the only one who could drive the car, take them into town for fried fish sandwiches or farther, to a bigger town, for a movie. What had she done to them? she wondered. They'd been getting along so well.

But the next day, all was forgotten, or if not forgotten, then at least forgiven. They huddled together on the front stoop while they drank their coffee, resting their heads on each other's shoulders, winding their arms in and around each other, shooing the dogs away when they wanted affection, linking elbows so their cups clinked.

Drought

The fields were full of purple lupine, upright and princely. The Heavenly Blue morning glories climbed the white clapboards of the house, and on the table, glasses etched with grapes held water and wine. Anna received a postcard from her mother showing fields of lavender in the south of France. There were no words, just a roughly drawn heart with an arrow through it, and a scratch-and-sniff patch. When scratched the patch smelled of lavender. She imagined her mother would bring her lavender sachets to tuck into her dresser drawers and slippery panties in a variety of purples. The tissue paper that wrapped them would rustle, would be a sheen of palest purple she wasn't sure of, turning it this way and that.

In town, the three girls sat on the library steps, waiting for it to open, Anna twirling a long strand of dirty hair around her finger. They'd been warned that the well might run dry should there be a week without heavy rain and so they'd stopped taking showers. Afternoon dips in the pond didn't really get them clean. Anna's clothes were dusty too, a spread of blueberry jam across the thigh of her jeans.

In the library, she ran her fingers along the spines, found another long, nineteenth-century novel to read. Now that she'd finished her mother's Agatha Christies and Nero Wolfes, she was working her way through all the Brontës. When the fog came in, she could imagine she was on the moors with Heathcliff. Alone in her room at night, with its one tiny window and low gabled ceiling, she could imagine she was Jane Eyre. What a romantic she was! Janice no less so, with her borrowed copy of Sylvia Plath. Emma–Beth too—she was reading Pasternak along with the Port Huron Statement. (How were any of them to know that its author Tom Hayden would divorce Jane Fonda and that she would go on to make workout videos and marry Ted Turner, billionaire founder of CNN—Hanoi Jane of all people, making workout videos!)

Anna loved her room, how she could close the door, the ancient, flowered wallpaper with its faded pansies, their yellow hearts and purple petals, the row of hooks from which she hung her jeans by their belt loops, her shirts by the tags. She draped skirts over the back of a chair, folded sweatshirts on its seat, nestled socks and underwear in a wicker basket. Another chair was her bedside table, and on it a mug of chamomile tea. She called the iron bedstead "the bed of the constant stranger" by which she meant she was always alone in it, and yet she loved it. This room, this whole house, some odd combination of bohemia, Anna reminded herself, and the decadent accoutrements of the moneyed class. Even if they were going to run out of water.

Everyday

The girls' routine—you know it: every morning, coffee and the dogs. Every afternoon, the pond. Every evening, a game of cards.

But they also sometimes did other things, like lie in the grass, tanning this way and that, or strip the old wallpaper in the kitchen, or fish for pollock off the pier.

Sunday night, they watched *Poldark* on Masterpiece Theater, the public station one of only two they could get on the little black-and-white TV. He was a champion for the underclass despite being thwarted in love. After the final episode, they wondered: What would they watch now? What would they discuss, as they had already exhausted all analyses of Ross Poldark's troubles?

Weeknights they watched the news on the other TV station, all about Carter's first year in office. What an old fogey! But at least he'd pardoned the draft dodgers—hundreds of thousands of unconditional pardons for draft evasion. The blackout back home. The capture of Son of Sam. Distant figures and words.

On Monday, they schlepped to the laundromat. On Friday, they baked bread. On Saturday, cleaned the bathroom, perhaps even scrubbing away mold with an old toothbrush.

At the end of June, it rained—off and on, a rain that did not relieve the heat. After that, a dry heat set in, replaced at intervals by a chilly mist that gathered in drops on their hair and fogged Janice's glasses.

Independence

Fourth of July and the night was clear. Anna had warned her friends it might be foggy, and then perhaps the fireworks would be postponed (a Fifth of July party, or even a Sixth, or a Seventh), or they'd just be hazy faint colors. "Oh there," someone would say, "I think," and point to where the fog turned pink, and everyone would laugh because, you know, Maine in the summer!

But no, this year it *was* clear, and they said "Boom" every time they saw a spring and spray of lights, the fireworks set off from an island in the harbor, white stars competing with white stars, red bursts the ruby love, green and blue, and their favorite, they all agreed, the sprinkling silver ones slowly raining down.

They had attended the parade: members of the local artist's colony dressed up as the huddled masses circling a gigantic puppet of Lady Liberty, the fire marshal, boys on bikes, a lobster princess, boats pulled behind tow trucks and stacked with lobster traps. For that one day, it seemed summer folk and year-round residents got along. Then they'd eaten pink salmon from the Penobscot River, green peas, red strawberries, opened the gray shells of steamed clams, and they'd swilled down lemonade. Then they watched the eight-year-olds hop a sack race, crying babies, and those idiot boys their own age throwing firecrackers into the street.

Now they shrieked, louder with every explosion, until their throats were sore, and they didn't care what anyone thought, didn't see everyone around them turn and look askance—who *are* those annoying girls?— and then the fireworks ended, three gigantic flowers—red, white, and blue—in quick succession, shattered like sequins from a dress, then silence.

"Huh," they said, not a question but just a huff of breath. Yes, they were high, having shared a joint down an alleyway with some boys they'd met at the lake.

Anna's Top Ten

They drove up and down country roads, singing "Donna Donna" in their best imitation Joan Baez voices. At the top of each rise, the car caught air. They had completely forgotten that the song is about a calf on its way to slaughter because they focused on the chorus: the laughing wind, the summer night, the swallow winging through the sky. They stuck their hands out the open windows, flipping through the slipstream. What was on the radio that summer? "Hotel California." The theme from *Rocky*. "Undercover Angel." "The Best of My Love." In Maine you could only get pop stations or the steady alternation of news and symphonies on NPR.

They were on their way to a bigger town to buy a record because back at the house they only had one that they listened to over and over, the Grateful Dead's *American Beauty*, imagining they were friends of the devil and staring at the red rose on the album cover or repeatedly reading the list of songs on the back.

At the store, they shuffled through racks, finally settling on another record from the early '70s, The Allman Brothers' *Eat a Peach*, because they only had money for one record and they'd heard about the picture inside. The cover was softly, deliciously pink, and they imagined sinking their teeth into it. The Clash had released their first album in April, the Sex Pistols had released "God Save the Queen" in May, and the Ramones had been around for years, playing in New York clubs these girls had barely heard of because they were looking back, already looking back, instead of forward.

On the way home, they sang "Box of Rain" and then Janice made up a song:

We will go down to Georgia
We'll bask in the sun
Always only fun.

That was the chorus. They knew it was terrible, but they sang it and sang it, emphasizing "will" and "bask" and "always" and "fun." They never made up any verses, but for the rest of the summer, whenever there was a moment of quiet, one of them would just sing "We *will*..." and the other two would start laughing until they peed a little in their pants. They had no idea why it was funny, just like they had no idea how sad that Joan Baez song was. They just were. It just was, like the crumbs caught in the cracks of the old oak table, the wild blueberries and sour cream for lunch, the doom of the parents' return, and the many moments they spent staring at the trippy landscape picture on the inside spread of that album cover. Back in the city, back at school, their senior year, they never said, "Hey do you remember that boy, that lake, the day we left the windows open and the sudden rain swooshed through the screens?" but sometimes when they passed in the halls, one would whisper "You *will*..." to another and wait for a gale of laughter.

Sex

One day at the pond, they found that boys had invaded their usual sunny spot, slouching in cut-off jeans, bare chested, long hairy toes gripping the edges of the rock while they tried (pretended?) to push each other into the water. Anna'd heard that lobstermen's boys, future lobstermen, never learned to swim: better to drown than freeze to death in the North Atlantic. If that was true, it added a special thrill to their game.

"Hey," one of them said, staring, and then common currency, common courtesy, he offered Emma a joint.

"You come here every day?" the boy said as she stepped back.

"You know we do," Anna said but didn't mean to flirt, not her.

Janice, more outgoing, said, "Yes, we've seen you too," although how could she have seen them since she was extremely blind without the wire-rimmed eyeglasses she took off to sunbathe and swim, and the boys usually parked themselves and their dogs across the pond? One of the dogs came up and sniffed her crotch right then. Anna's old sheepdog did not reciprocate, instead growled before backing away to lie in the shade. Old scaredy cat! They all laughed, boys and girls together.

The group of boys kept growing, shrinking, an indeterminate number appearing from and disappearing into the wooded path that ran up and down the lakeshore. They flicked ash, hip checked each other so that they almost fell off the rock, and tossed empty beer cans into the water, where they drifted with the current down to the end of the pond closest to the garbage dump. The girls found this most ironically appropriate but not really funny as they'd skipped school to rid Central Park of trash on the first Earth Day and every one since.

Emma said, "Hey, don't you swim here?" hands on her hips, an angry glare.

The boys chuckled back at her, one mimicking her in a high mincing tone, and another muttering "summer jerks" not quite under his breath.

Anna heard him and knew she'd been right to be sort of scared to say anything. Not scared that the boys would get mad or hit them or anything, but scared that the boys would think the girls were fools, even though she knew they were NOT fools. She thought, well, it is their place, their town, their lake. No hard feelings, though, as it turned out, because when she tuned back in, they were being invited to a party and the tallest boy was lovingly stroking Janice's long hair.

That night, Emma (after Emma Goldman) crawled into bed with Anna. "Why did you say we'd go to that party? Now we either have to go or never go back to the pond."

"It'll just be for a little while. We can leave whenever you want," Anna said, even though she didn't know why she wanted to go. Maybe she'd been infected by Janice's bubbly excitement.

And so they went to the party at the Sugar Shack, presided over by the guy Elm who lived there, a man in his thirties entertaining teenagers. Shadeless bulbs hung in the kitchen and living room, people tumbled up and down the steps and in and out of the one bedroom. The girls sucked in some hot marijuana smoke, drank warm beer from cans, felt their asses get rubbed, and thanked god they didn't have to try to make conversation because the music was so loud, the hard twang of Lynyrd Skynrd's "Free Bird" and "Sweet Home Alabama." So high, Anna thought, we're so far north we're south again. She hated these people. But then she felt guilty—it was their town after all and we're just summer jerks. What right do I have to judge?

But there was one boy with long blond hair and a pale face. She fantasized he would throw pebbles against her bedroom window later, and she would go down to him, and they would talk and talk and he would turn out to be sensitive and smart, and he'd never realized he liked to read until she gave him *The Lord of the Rings*. She imagined the conversation they would never have about Ents and the sorrow the Ents felt about the disappearance of their Entwives. She stared at him until he noticed and came over. He was taller than she'd expected and he said "Oh, really" perfectly. He leaned over her, one hand on the wall next to her head and the other . . . OK, she knew this scene and where it could go, where she would go, and she did. Years later, she would remember him and realize he actually looked like Orlando Bloom who played Legolas in all the *Lord of the Rings* movies and who had—funny— actually been born in 1977. Or maybe seeing Orlando Bloom play Legolas had changed her memories of that party and that boy.

When Anna rejoined the party, Janice was making out with Elm. Later, Janice smelled musty of pot and sour of beer and fishy of lobster. And Emma was sitting in a corner on Andrew's lap. (Who was he? Anna wondered. She had never seen him before.) She herself smelled of ash and grass, but he'd cum before he was inside her, so she was still, technically, a virgin. The next day at the pond, and the next and next after that, until it was time to drive Janice and Emma to the bus terminal and pick Anna's parents up at the airport, none of the boys appeared.

One day, she's going through some dusty cardboard boxes, looking for her mother's death certificate, which she doesn't find. She finds a notebook from 1977 instead and in it, along with a record of that summer in Maine, sees a tally of every time she got catcalled by a construction worker on the streets of Manhattan. She had also written about every couple she saw on the street, in the post office, the well matched and the mismatched, the ones tied to each other with invisible rope, the ones fighting. "A boy and a girl passed," she wrote, "and I had the strongest wish that I had a boyfriend. Oh well!" Should she have been afraid of those guys, their hoots and whistles? She does not remember being afraid. Even the guy jerking off as he walked out of the subway station at Park Avenue South and Twenty-Third Street didn't scare her—that was just gross. Apparently, she had bopped down Third Avenue as if she owned it—or that's what a friend of her mother's reported. She might have been a stupid teenager but she finds the innocence alluring.

Another Wave

Anna never thought it would turn out like this, this whiskey-stained world. She had no idea, sitting on the stoop of the summerhouse with her friends as they all drank their morning coffee, that the ice caps would melt and that the seas would rise and that the rocky Maine beaches would be covered, and then the meadows and the sloping hills and the blueberry fields, and then the road leading from the post office to the grocery store that sold the best donuts (crispy on the outside and soft on the inside, chocolate and evenly coated with sugar crystals) and the antique store where every year she bought lace-edged linens that she never used, and that eventually that very front stoop would drown. The house itself had been sold long before even though her mother's ashes were interred in the cement walls of the low-ceilinged basement and her father's ashes scattered over the swamp out back. In grade school, she'd laughed at the fifteenth-century idiots who thought there was a Northwest Passage through which they could sail from Europe, over the top of the world, and then down again to Asia for spices. They hadn't realized that the entire Arctic Ocean was layered thick with ice, but the world was now quick nearing the time when sailing over the pole would be commonplace, when kids would expect dust storms, wildfires, multiple category five hurricanes every season and wouldn't miss polar bears because they'd never have seen one, not even in a zoo.

Now her house is filled with radioactive dust bunnies, the fish farm pens filled with inedible two-headed salmon she hopes won't escape into the surrounding sea, wildfire smoke caught in her hair. Books crumble when she picks them up, and the electronic ones are never available from the library. "Your hold is number ninety-five on twenty-eight copies," the message reads. She sees her old friends, Emma and Janice, on a trip back home, or thinks she does. Is it really them? It is impossible to reenter that world.

Last Week, New Year

By the road, the last time from the hospital, under the surge of blue mottled clouds driven from the northwest, over the Hudson—a cold wind insisted, so strange for September. At long last, Anna was an orphan. Her chest expanded at the thought: father gone, mother gone, dead from complications of a broken hip at the age of eighty-six, short of the 101 she'd hoped to reach. Anna had been glad to see the old thing go, along with her attempts at matchmaking, her reminders to attend shul on the High Holy Days, her compulsive cleaning, her constant questioning, and her weekly dinners: oily potato latkes, gelatinous gefilte fish, galuptzi with the soft cabbage leaves surrounding a too-sweet mixture of beef and rice, tasteless angel food cake—her mother had never been the best cook.

Finally an orphan, Anna had buried her mother and organized the funeral, attended by herself and her mother's remaining cronies—old biddy birds, her mother would have called them with a laugh, who stumbled in on their walkers, or were wheeled in by aides, women wearing white and carrying, in their voluminous purses, books of crossword puzzles. In the evening, after the funeral and one celebratory glass of Prosecco, Anna realized she had exactly a week to clear out the apartment before the landlord brought the wrecking ball to knock this building down and put up a new one, something huge and covered with yellow brick, something clean and stepless, with an elevator. At the end of the week, the High Holy Days would come too, and when the shofar was blown, Anna would be there, attending shul for the first time in many years and standing for the Kaddish. Promise me, her mother had said in the hospital.

She had one week to clear out the apartment before the landlord brought the wrecking ball, and she only had that because she'd begged. The apartment was rent controlled, and although the landlord had often offered Anna's mother, the last tenant in the building, money to move out, she'd always refused, asking rhetorically, "Where can I move with that kind of money?" Promise me, her mother had said, promise me that you'll throw nothing away. To throw away would have been easy: rent a dumpster and cast everything out the window.

Her mother had been living in the rent-controlled apartment for over fifty years, Anna's entire life, living there with Anna, and Anna's father until he died, and with numerous cats and dogs, all of whom were long gone. And so Anna had the apartment—the building—to herself, despite the mice she heard scratching in the walls at night, or the roaches that ran for the kitchen corners when she turned on the light. Really, it was just her and all this crap she needed to get rid of, all this crap that wasn't all crap, of course, because then it would have been easy to throw away, grown beards of dust as it had since her mother's move to the hospital. Instead, she stood with her hands on her hips, considering the antique cherry loveseat, the first editions of Saul Bellow novels, teacups that might be Sèvres, an Italian tapestry that looked old enough to be important, and then there were the sentimental items: her parents' wedding rings, her old report cards, photos of unidentifiable aunts and uncles, collars from her old dogs and some of their hair, a black scallop shell from a long-ago trip to the Lido, beads she had strung, letters from one grandparent to another in a language she couldn't read—all things she couldn't now, she supposed, throw away.

For now, Anna had the apartment—the building—to herself, despite the roaches and the mice rustling in the dust under the living room furniture, no neighbors, husband or children, no pets or partners. Anna had never married—why? she wondered, because opportunities had presented themselves although she'd never met anyone she couldn't see tossing away or tossing her away. And why could she not manage to throw away that shell from the Mediterranean or the old report card on which some teacher had scribbled, "Anna seems to prefer to spend time alone"? Maybe if she had married, she would be divorced by now, single again but with a singular type of failure attached to her—at least she imagines it that way, although her divorced friends like to say it's a triumph.

Anna's mother had been widowed young, had remained widowed, and although she'd often wondered aloud why Anna had never married, she'd also liked to pretend they were single girlfriends, Anna remembered. Maybe this year, she would have gone to Rosh Hashanah or Yom Kippur services with her mother—but no, who was she kidding? No marriage to toss, but instead, this sin she'd cast into the sea, this wrongdoing she'd send into the wilderness with the goat, this transgression: that she had listened to her mother with only her outer ear. She couldn't imagine she'd be granted a clean slate no matter how many times she knocked her chest, her chest now filled with something strange, and she turned her head away from the half-filled carton of dusty books on the floor and saw a doe bound down the hallway—an instant of dark eyes, too-large ears, a brown flank, the final flick of a white tail, and a whiff of something animal.

Maybe this year, she would have gone to services with her mother—but no, she couldn't even kid herself about that. Her chest contracted at the thought: father gone, mother gone, but my, how her mother had remained beautiful up to the day she fell down the stairs— just those two stairs from kitchen to living room—and broke her hip, still wearing a slip and nylons and her lipstick still perfect when the paramedics came. Anna couldn't imagine she'd be granted a clean slate no matter how many times she knocked her chest, and when she looked into the hallway, she expected to see the doe again running away, but instead, she saw a bunny resting its dusty paws at the edge of the carpet, watching her with sparkling and inquisitive brown eyes, twitching its dusty nose, pricking its dusty ears, and when she got up, it followed her, hopping closer, loping closer, until she could feel the warmth bristle through its dirty fur, and it finally, as she stood at the kitchen counter to open a can of soup, rested its head against her ankle. Under the surge of blue mottled clouds driven from the northwest, a cold wind insisted— so strange for September—hit her mother's windows noiselessly, and then the clouds brought rain.

Inebriate of Air

Wedding Plans

BRIDE: a virgin, of course. Drunk on anticipation, the guests laugh boisterously. We make predictions about the first sexual encounter, and some even place bets (position, duration), though it's hard to imagine how such bets might be settled.

DATE: midsummer's eve. The sun stays up for hours and hours, long past her usual bedtime, as we also stay up past ours.

FLOWERS: blue foxgloves and white starflowers, yellow buttercups aplenty. Her mother says, Are you sure about the buttercups? They last such a short time. Her father says, Are you sure about the foxglove? Could be poisonous.

WEDDING DRESS: deep V-neck and winglike sleeves; a sash of silver wrapped round and round the bride's tiny waist, kimono style; a flowing skirt—white, of course, then glimmering gray and pink; the bodice beaded with pearls, each one sewn on separately with golden thread. Married or not, in love or not, we covet her—or it.

TUXEDO: lapis lazuli—not really, just the color.

MUSIC: Vivaldi for the ceremony, the dulcet strains of Spring and Summer. During the reception: Kisses Sweeter Than Wine, Ol' Blue Eyes crooning The Summer Wind, the repeated throbbing notes of Janis Joplin's Summertime.

DRINK: dewdrops—imagine champagne muddled with purple plum, in glasses rimmed with nacre.

FOOD: we need none, sated with love.

DANCES: not reels—more like waltzes, on the portable dance floor workmen have placed in the meadow behind the inn. Though reel we do.

WEDDING CAKE: angel food layered with divinity, topped with ceramic seraphs. We see the bride lick fondant from a wing.

WEDDING FAVOR: an oyster shell, containing a pearl.

RELEASE: white butterflies and blue-chested hummingbirds imported from Brazil. The bride and groom walk away through grass just beginning to dew, under maple leaves blooming a tender green—if leaves can be said to bloom, blessed by a blue night sky—midnight to the east and cobalt to the west where the sun has only just set.

Questions

What do the bride and groom do once they're finally alone, no longer drunk on champagne and wedding gifts, tossing tissue paper at each other and giggling as they unwrap plate after useless plate? Inebriation doesn't last, that's why we write poems about it. Eventually, they will wake up, hungover, with ribbons knotted in her hair and frosting stuck to his chin. I'll not write what happens next, except to say she doesn't lick the frosting off; he wipes it away roughly with the sheet, embarrassed. Let's leave them, avert our eyes from the first time they touch the soft skin above each other's waists, afraid to move their hands.

What's the after in their happily ever? Have her parents guessed correctly, with their worries about the flowers—a short-lived and poisonous marriage? I could invent one, or a happy one, or dull, or long, or violent, or amusing, but their marriage remains mysterious, closed like the bedroom door on Sunday mornings. Nor will their children surmise their secrets, even after their parents are dead, their mother first becoming a skinny old woman and their father a fat old man who still proudly wears the same size pants as the day he married but now they're buckled under his gut. What secrets do they have, the bride and groom? Secret ways of inflicting pleasure and lavishing pain that only they know, that are only effective when applied to each other, and that I cannot even guess at here.

Letter

Dear Mother (the bride writes, no longer a bride),

Please forgive my long delay in answering your last note—and I've so much to tell from this far country. I never knew the world could be so enchanting—pearl gleaming and golden, the children's little faces when I rouse them in the morning, and out they run to lick dew from the grass with their pink tongues like cats or snails. "Why does the dog eat bees?" they ask. "Don't they sting his poor mouth?" They jump and spin. The baby toddles after her older brothers. Later, I lie on the grass with them, certainly ruining my skirts, and listen as they turn the clouds into dragons, castles, and ponies. When their father comes from the city on Friday afternoons and scoops them up, I lie there still, gaze up at dragonflies that hover in a mating dance (I hope you don't blush to see me write such things), breathe deep of foxglove and clover and wait for the sun to shift west and spread the shade of the maple tree over me.

I read of my sister's wedding with enthusiasm and was gladdened to hear of the pleasure our gift brought her. The blue pottery is native to these parts, the color a quality of the clay dug from the cliffs here rather than a glaze. I wish my sister the greatest happiness and will be most pleased to meet her husband, Mr. B, when I return home. I must inform you, though, that such a trip will not be possible, at least until next summer, for the journey by ship is long and the boys start their schooling in the fall. Soon the autumn mists will come here like little gray foxes, and the leaves turn, and the snows fall, and you would not want us to miss all that, would you?

Your daughter, Emily

Diary

Fourteen years later, the bride's daughter, Jennifer, writes in her diary: *Now I know what they're all going on about!* She seals her knowledge with a red lipstick print.

Jennifer spends her high school years avoiding her older brothers, partying, fucking, coasting her bike down the dark streets by the warehouses late at night, where one light might mark a steel-shuttered door. She likes, when she's had a few beers, to choose a boy and wrap his hair around her thumb and pull his head toward her own and kiss him until she forgets everything except the shape of his teeth and the gravity of his tongue and the sweet/salt balance of his saliva. The summer after graduation, she takes the only job she can get—given her poor performance in school—companion for a bedridden old lady who lives on the outskirts of town. For years, the girl has slept through the days, woken only at sunset, but her job requires her to wake early, and strangely, she finds it no burden, for the old lady has wisely removed the curtains from all the windows of her house. Indeed, the girl barely sleeps at all now, wakes to the hummingbirds' hum and whir. At dawn, she sees pearl-like light, dew on the rosemary, and later, when she wheels the old lady outside in her chair, sun on the buttercups. They sit in the middle of the garden, and the old lady tells her: there's red-orange tiger lily, that's good for restlessness. Yes, dear, stew the bulbs and sleep tonight. There is poppy, that's for anxiety, and chrysanthemum cures colds. Pink rose petals, chewed, ease depression. Foxglove is good for the heart.

Jennifer abandons her diary, friend through her long adolescence. She spends every spare moment out of doors. She even sleeps outside the last night of summer, and before sleeping she asks the hippie farmer neighbor to join her in a reel. She's been looking, she says, into ways of making dandelion wine. Will he share his recipe? She's seen him drinking something from a big brown jug, and though he argues that it's only ginger water, she persists, dancing with him, teasing, dancing, even under the stars, even in the cold grass by the river's edge and the mud there traced with snail tracks. It all enthralls her—day and night, wet and dry, sun and moon, the bee and the butterfly. You don't need wine, he says, catching her under the willow tree. Finally, toward dawn, he says, I can't help you, and pats her ass one last time. Even I need to rest. The animals need care.

In the evening, after a day spent ragged in the hedges and burnished by the sun, eating berries with muddy fingers, she returns to the old lady who has managed to get herself into bed, using her last strength perhaps. They watch the sunset together through the bedroom window, a particularly bloody sunset, and then, through the other window, they watch the rise of the harvest moon, so large and orange it looks as if it might swallow them up or roll down out of the sky and crush them, so large and close the girl thinks she could reach through the window and touch it—or no, maybe if she just climbed up to the roof of the house. The old lady gives a deep sigh. She believes that in the morning she will be dead, but in the morning, when he sees no smoke rising from their chimney, the farmer comes over and finds her gently asleep, under a soft quilt, her breath frosting the first autumn air, tissues and water glass placed lovingly within reach on the bedside table. He finds the girl too, her back broken by the maple limb she landed on when she fell from the roof.

Letter

Dearest Mother,

I regret writing with distressing news so soon after hearing of my beloved father's passing, but we have faced sorrow here too. Your darling Jennifer, your only granddaughter . . . (Here the letter dissolves into a jumble of tear-streaked words, a lock of the girl's hair twisted into a delicate bow and fashioned into a brooch, a newspaper clipping describing the local fire fighters' attempts to revive her. It only emerges a page later to describe how the bride and her husband have invited the old lady, their daughter's employer, to live with them.) For dear mother, in her sweetness and kindness, she reminds me of you. And as the distance is so great between us, and as I am denied the pleasure of your company and of caring for you in these last years, I will avail myself of this opportunity to provide comfort to her.

Your loving daughter, Emily

Coda

Sprays of orange leaves, red holly berries, chartreuse hellebores, golden daffodils to decorate the room. Clean water to drink in a green glass that glistens like mother-of-pearl. The old lady lasts through the winter and spring, and dies when the bluebottles rise to swarm in the next summer's heat. The bride holds her hand as she goes, holds her hand through the last breaths that rattle on and on, then watches the blood drain from her face. An hour later, the old lady's back is still warm.

Forest

Winter

Inside each of us is a dark reservoir. Sleeping, the old woman curls around the baby, the tight shell of a walnut. The cabin contains a still life: brown table and chairs, wool mittens hung to dry, earthenware dishes, bread, lentil soup. When the baby wakes, the old woman takes her to the fire and rubs her hands in its warmth. They sing—alto, babble, bah bah of sheep through the wall.

One day, the old woman finds two ancient quarters behind the rocking chair cushions and decides to buy a treat in town. Patiently she waits for the snow to stop falling, and when it does, she straps snowshoes to her feet and the baby to her back and walks out into the blue afternoon. Her brown cloak moves quietly between the trees, from shadow to light and back again, and a red woolen cap sits on the baby's head, attracting birds that come to peck at it, looking for something to eat. It has been so cold for so long that no icicles hang from the branches and the streams are silent, rivulets and waterfalls frozen into a decadence of ice; it is so cold now that the baby's breath freezes and furs immediately on her scarf. Where the sun shines, the snow is blinding, but under the trees, blue deepens to a darkness bordering on gray. On Main Street, the only store is out of brownies, cookies, chocolate bars, and cocoa powder—and just as well for the old woman had no milk to make it with. Instead, the merchant offers the old woman Nutella, just arrived from France, a spread of chocolate and hazelnuts, which, he assures her, will turn any slice of toast into dessert, and she takes it, her mouth already watering and the baby already reaching over her shoulder for the jar.

On the way home, trees creak, ice cracks, a chickadee whistles. She's been warned she might run into bandits. Instead, she points out the tracks of a snowshoe hare, a polar wolf, and a rare white squirrel. At home, the baby licks Nutella off her finger and scrapes with her tiny sharp teeth. From the bed, they watch flame shadows until they fall asleep, sweetness still on their tongues.

Spring

Will plot necessitate that something more happen than a frog emerging from a pond? In the forest, moss vibrates and new leaves haze the trees. A girl clutches the week's groceries in a string bag and watches the platoon marching through town. She is old enough to love but young enough to get in trouble. Instead of turning home, she follows them, and for an instant the soldier at the end of the line turns to look at her.

Across the street, another woman leans against her porch railing and watches too, resting one hand on her belly to feel the quickening. Could the baby's father be the one with a blond scruffy beard or the one with dark hair and blue eyes or him, the quick one with his loose loping stride—because she's been with all of them. For lunch, she eats fresh peas with mint, a lettuce wedge with green goddess dressing, and she can't be still. She sits down, slurps soup, gets up again, peers out the window, scoops peas and spears lettuce leaves and chews bread while she straightens the newspaper, takes out the trash, and opens her mail with a paring knife. Soon the men will march into a foreign city, a big city with an opera house, museums devoted to art and commerce, a symphony hall, a botanical garden where every plant is labeled with its Latin name, and they will walk among those wonders, bumping shoulders and telling jokes. (Pause.) She knows she is a green-eyed monster; inside her the baby swims laps, spirals, turns and returns between her heart and her pubic bone, between her liver and her spleen.

That night the soldiers camp by a stream, and the girl beds down nearby. Did the young soldier come to her and touch her lip with just one finger? More? In the morning, she hears nothing: the army is gone.

From the top of the rise, she sees the platoon below, readying the howitzers.

Summer

In the late afternoon, showers briefly ease the torpor. The melons have ripened too quickly—first split, then rot. Foolishly, she planted the vegetable patch out in the field. Far from the house, the sun there is relentless. And she hates lugging water from the spigot in the yellow plastic bucket.

She much prefers lying in the hammock strung between the black locust trees, attempting to count the individual leaflets along each stem. Watching the grass grow? her mother asks when she comes out, bringing a wet glass of lemonade and slices of watermelon, and swinging the hammock when she sits down. The mother eyes her daughter's belly: she's been watching it grow all summer, although she has yet to say anything—at least anything direct—for despite this respite at home, her daughter is old enough and wealthy enough to take care of herself and a child. Should the girl's father still have been alive, he would have ranted, screeched blame, threatened disinheritance or a shotgun marriage, and her daughter would have laughed and asked how many of the possible fathers she should marry. Her mother would like to know for sure whether her daughter is pregnant, although she has to admit to herself that she's already pretty darn sure. She would like to know if her daughter knows the sex of the child, because she would like to start planning (names, sweater and cap colors other than sunflower or pale green, nursery decorations, childcare plans, baby food brands, cloth diapers versus disposables, etc.) but she dares not ask. Instead, they clatter ice cubes and eat melon, wiping the juice from their cheeks with the backs of their hands.

Down in the forest, preteen girls run between the trees. Their bare white torsos shine, and their golden hair flags out behind them. A hand grabs a trunk. Then a whoop of delight rings back up the hill. Aspens shake their leaves.

Over the mountain, gray clouds mask the orange moon. The wind brings down a whoosh of leaves. Holly berries and prickly buckeye conkers blot the forest floor. Last sun meets first frost. In her chest, the woman rages, in her heart.

Or is it in her head, a constant screaming command to her and to her mother lying bedridden in the cottage? She's been lying there for months, her breath growing shallower and shallower, until now she just gurgles and spits, and yet she seems unaware of this. Her teeth are relaxed, allowing her lips to take on the shape of a smile, and her eyes are soft, and her fingers have uncurled. Rage! her daughter mouths silently, aware all the while of the visiting white-hatted nurse in the background, straightening a table cloth or washing a cup or readying a hypodermic with morphine. The woman wants her mother to rage and not to rage, to shout and to be silent, to toss and tumble and throw her blankets off and to do the crossword puzzle with one pencil in her hand and another tucked behind her ear, as she sits up in a silvery satin bedjacket against dove gray pillows. If her mother doesn't rage, it's easier to care for her once the nurse leaves for the day, but if she does rage, it means she's not going to die yet. Even if she never followed her mother's advice, she now misses her mother's mentorship: the appraising glance, the plucking fingers, the deft instruction, the withering sigh, the shining example.

Is it possible to describe silence without using a metaphor? *Not* silence clamps down or settles. The baby holds something in her fist. What is it? Between her fingers, light streams out.

MAYA SONENBERG

is professor of English in the Creative Writing Program
at the University of Washington. Her previous collections of short stories
include *Cartographies* (winner of the Drue Heinz Literature Prize)
and *Voices from the Blue Hotel.* Her fiction and nonfiction have appeared
in *Fairy Tale Review*, *Web Conjunctions*, *DIAGRAM*, *New Ohio Review*,
The Literarian, *Hotel Amerika*, and elsewhere.

CPSIA information can be obtained
at www.ICGtesting.com
Printed in the USA
LVHW081126030822
725063LV00014B/1040